The April Rainers

By Anthea Fraser

The April Rainers
Six Proud Walkers
The Nine Bright Shiners
Death Speaks Softly
Pretty Maids All in a Row
A Shroud for Delilah

ANTHEA FRASER

The April Rainers

A CRIME CLUB BOOK
DOUBLEDAY
New York   London   Toronto   Sydney   Auckland

A CRIME CLUB BOOK
PUBLISHED BY DOUBLEDAY
a division of Bantam Doubleday Dell Publishing Group, Inc.
666 Fifth Avenue, New York, New York 10103

DOUBLEDAY and the portrayal of a man
with a gun are trademarks of Doubleday,
a division of Bantam Doubleday Dell
Publishing Group, Inc.

Library of Congress Cataloging-in-Publication Data

Fraser, Anthea.
    The April rainers/Anthea Fraser.—1st ed. in the U.S.A.
        p.   cm.
    "A Crime Club book."
    I. Title.
PR6056.R286A84   1990
823'.914—dc20   89-23615
CIP

ISBN 0-385-41088-3
Copyright © 1989 by Anthea Fraser
All Rights Reserved
Printed in the United States of America
May 1990
First Edition in the United States of America

BVG

GREEN GROW THE RUSHES-O

I'll sing you one-o!
(*Chorus*) Green grow the rushes-o!
    What is your one-o?
One is one and all alone and evermore shall be so.

I'll sing you two-o!
(*Chorus*) Green grow the rushes-o!
    What are your two-o?
Two, two, the lily-white Boys, clothéd all in green-o,
(*Chorus*) One is one and all alone and evermore shall be
    so.

I'll sing you three-o!
(*Chorus*) Green grow the rushes-o!
    What are your three-o?
Three, three the Rivals,
(*Chorus*) Two, two, the lily-white Boys,
    clothed all in green-o,
One is one and all alone and evermore shall be so.

Four for the Gospel-makers.

Five for the Symbols at your door.

Six for the six proud Walkers.

Seven for the seven Stars in the sky.

Eight for the April Rainers.

Nine for the nine bright Shiners.

Ten for the ten Commandments.

Eleven for the Eleven that went up to heaven.

Twelve for the twelve Apostles.

The April Rainers

1

THAT THURSDAY in early October did not start well for Webb. The telephone roused him just before six, and he dragged himself from the depths of sleep to hear the station sergeant's voice in his ear.

"Sorry to wake you, sir. We've a suspicious death in Rankin Close. Number five."

Webb rubbed his eyes with his free hand, squinted at the clock and sighed. "Any details, Andy?"

"The milkman found him outside his back door. Steve Dacre went over—he's just phoned in. Says he's contacted Docs Pringle and Stapleton."

"Right." Webb was already swinging his feet to the floor. "Get on to Sergeant Jackson and tell him I'll pick him up in ten minutes. Then phone the SOCOs. Rankin Close, you said?"

"That's right, sir. It's that bungalow development off Rankin Road—only half a dozen houses."

"I know the one. Thanks, Andy." Webb dropped the phone and went through to the bathroom. A domestic murder by the sound of it, he reflected, sluicing his face with cold water. Unlikely to be a random attack in a backwater like that.

As he turned into Broadminster Road, he could see Jackson's slight figure waiting under the street lamp outside his gate.

"Nice start to the day, guv!" he said cheerfully, pulling the car door shut behind him.

"Wonderful. Bloke outside his own back door. Dacre thinks we should see him."

"Know who he is?"

"No, but the milkman will. He found him."

They saw the milkfloat as they turned into the Close. It was in front of the last house on the left, with Dacre's car behind it. A light was on in the house, defiantly illuminating the porch and a short stretch of path in the surrounding darkness. Around it, its neighbours slept on, unaware of the drama in their midst, and the only watcher was a ginger cat, who surveyed them without interest from a garage roof.

Webb and Jackson got out of the car into the cold early morning. A heavy dew dampened the pavement and beaded the grass on the verge. An hour or so, and the sun would dry it.

PC Dacre came to the gate to meet them, accompanied by a thin, apprehensive-looking young man.

"Morning, sir. This is Mr. Brodie, who found the deceased."

The milkman, barely in his twenties, was shivering as much from shock as from the chill in the air.

"Can you tell us what happened, Mr. Brodie?"

"I just walked round the corner of the house, same as always, and there he was. Got the fright of my life, I can tell you. I thought he'd had a heart attack so I bent down, like, to see if I could do anything. But when I got a proper look at him—" He gagged, put a hand over his mouth. "Sorry," he mumbled.

"You'll know who he is, since he's one of your customers?"

"Yeah. The name's Baxter."

"You're quite sure it's him? You didn't just assume it, because this is his house?"

"It's him all right."

"Did you knock on the door for help?"

"No point—he's the only one here."

"When you bent down, did you touch him in any way, to make sure he was dead?"

"I didn't need to." Brodie's voice shook again. Webb glanced questioningly at the police constable, and he nodded confirmation.

"So you rang us. Where from?"

"The phone box in Rankin Road. It's only round the corner, but my legs were that wobbly I nearly didn't make it."

They turned as another car drew up at the gate, and Dr. Pringle unfolded his long body from behind the steering wheel.

Webb said, "Sergeant, take Mr. Brodie back to the station. I'm sure he could do with a cup of tea while he gives his statement."

"But what about my round?" Brodie interrupted. "The boss won't half give me stick if the deliveries aren't done."

"You can phone him from the police station. We won't keep you any longer than necessary." He turned to the police surgeon. "I'll come and take a look with you, Alec; I've only just got here myself."

The side-gate stood open and on the path immediately beyond it lay a pool of milk spiked with shards of broken glass. Stepping over it, the two men surveyed the scene. Behind the bungalow a narrow garden stretched some hundred feet, with boundary fences on three sides. A narrow concrete path led along the back of the house, and the inert form lay sprawled across it. Pringle had a torch ready, but the body was eerily spotlit by light seeping through the thin window blind.

The dead man was heavily built and lay on his side with his head towards the house. His face was horribly distorted, with the tongue forced out, eyes open and staring, and blood-flecked froth staining nose and mouth. No wonder the milkman was upset; death by strangulation was a gruesome sight.

Unusual, too, in such circumstances; a quick knife-thrust or the ubiquitous blunt instrument was more the norm.

Pringle moved forward, squatting by the prone figure. After a couple of minutes, Webb said tentatively, "You reckon he's been here all night?"

"Aye, I'd say so. He's stiff, and the ground's dry beneath him." He glanced up at the house. "Is anyone inside?"

"No; the milkman says he lived alone."

The doctor pursed his lips. "Well, since he's wearing an anorak, I'd say he was followed home. He'd probably left the lights on to make the house look occupied."

"Or he might have been indoors, and slipped on the jacket to investigate a noise outside. In which case—" Webb wrapped a handkerchief round his hand and tried the door handle. It withstood his pressure. "End of that theory. But if he'd just come home, why not go to the front door?"

Pringle shrugged and straightened. "Some folk always use the back. Or perhaps he heard a noise round here as he was putting the car away. Pushed open the side-gate, disturbed a would-be burglar, and—wham."

"There's no sign of attempted break-in. Still, once the SOCOs have finished, we'll get a look at his pockets. If he has car keys on him, you could be right."

"Mr. Baxter?" An anxious voice reached them from the other side of the fence. "Is that you? Whatever's happening?"

Webb walked across and, stepping on a convenient brick, looked over the fence. A small woman stood there in dressing-gown and slippers, a gauze scarf wound round her head. She gave a little gasp and took a step backwards and Webb said quickly, "Don't be alarmed, ma'am—we're the police. I'm afraid Mr. Baxter's had an accident."

"What is it?" she quavered, a hand going to her throat. "What's happened to him?"

Webb hesitated. "Is anyone with you, ma'am?"

"My husband, yes."

"All right if I come round and have a word with you both?"

"Now?" Her voice rose. "But it's only half-past six—we're not even dressed!"

"Don't worry about that. Actually," he added, reverting to the everyday to reassure her, "a cup of tea would be very welcome."

"Well—all right then."

Webb nodded his thanks. "I'll be round in five minutes."

When he returned to the front of the house, the pathologist had arrived, and, hard on his heels, the Scenes of Crime Officers. And now some of the fuss had penetrated the closed curtains of Rankin Close. One of them twitched as he glanced across the road, and a light or two had blossomed in previously dark windows. PC Dacre was still at the gate, preserving the scene.

"I'm going next door for a chat, Steve," Webb told him as the other men moved down the drive. "If I get the chance, I'll slip you a cuppa to keep you going."

"Thanks, sir. None too warm, is it?"

"The sun'll be up soon—that'll help."

Webb paused to study the small close. As Andy Fenton had said, it was a development of six bungalows, and beyond number five the road ended in a gravel turning-place. The killer, then, must have left the same way he'd come. In any case, if he'd arrived by car, he was more likely to have parked in Rankin Road than risk driving into a deadend. And *had* Baxter disturbed a burglar, or was he followed home? Suppose he'd been flashing money around in a pub? Again, a search of his pockets might provide the answer.

A light flicked on in the porch of the next-door house, and Webb, taking the hint, quickened his footsteps. The door opened as he reached it, and he found himself facing a middle-aged man with tousled hair and a less than welcoming expression. That he had dressed hurriedly and with bad grace was indicated by his wrongly buttoned shirt.

"Good morning, sir. I'm sorry to disturb you at this hour. Chief Inspector Webb, CID."

"Grogan," said the man sullenly. "I suppose you'd better come in, though why you need to see us, I can't imagine."

As Webb stepped into the hall, Mrs. Grogan appeared from the kitchen. She too had dressed, and a hasty touch of powder and lipstick had been applied. Unconventional though the hour may be, appearances must be kept up.

"In here, Chief Inspector."

She ushered him into the living-room, which extended the full depth of the house. Yesterday's paper lay on the floor, and the cushions were still dented from the previous evening. On a side table stood a couple of mugs and two plates with crumbs of cheese on them. Mrs. Grogan tutted, swept them up and carried them out to the kitchen.

"Now," Grogan said impatiently, as she came bustling back with a tea-tray, "what the devil's this all about?"

But first, Webb asked if he might take a mug to the man on the gate, a request Grogan allowed somewhat grudgingly. As he came back into the room, they both looked up at him expectantly. He took his own cup off the tray and settled in the chair indicated.

"Before I go into details, I'd be grateful if you'd tell me what you know about Mr. Baxter. Was he a friend of yours?"

The Grogans, exchanging glances, hadn't noticed his use of the past tense. The man cleared his throat. "No offence, Chief Inspector, but we make it a rule not to discuss our neighbours' affairs. We respect their privacy and expect them to respect ours."

"Very worthy, sir," said Webb drily. "However, these are special circumstances. Mr. Baxter is dead."

"Dead?" They spoke in unison, staring at him unbelievingly. Mrs. Grogan put her cup down before her suddenly shaking hands could spill it. "Oh my goodness! That's terrible! What happened?"

"Easy, Beth," said her husband, as though to a bucking

mare. She subsided against the cushions and he added to Webb, "Heart, was it?"

"No, Mr. Grogan," Webb said deliberately. "It was murder."

Mrs. Grogan gave a faint shriek and her husband moved to join her on the sofa, taking her hand. The shock had banished his grumpy sleepiness and he was fully alert.

"I think I've said enough for you to appreciate the gravity of the situation," Webb continued, "so I'd be grateful for a few details. How long has Mr. Baxter lived next door?"

Grogan moistened his lips, still trying to absorb the news. "About three years, I suppose. Since soon after the bungalows were built."

"And he lived alone, I hear."

"Well, for the last six weeks, yes."

Webb's eyes narrowed. "And before that?"

"They were all there. His wife and the kids."

"So what happened?"

Grogan's eyes fell. "That's why we're careful what we say. Heaven knows, there's been enough gossip. The fact is, Chief Inspector, he was a violent man; used to beat her up, and the kids, too, I shouldn't wonder. Anyway, when the poor woman could take no more, she reported him and he was taken to court." His voice hardened, became angry. "And because he'd got a fast-talking lawyer, those namby-pamby magistrates let him off with a fine. So what happens? When he turns up at the house again, his wife takes an overdose."

That, Webb thought bitterly, was all he needed. The whole neighbourhood would be hostile to this man.

"What happened to the children?"

"Her sister took them, poor little devils."

"Have you her name and address?"

"I'm afraid not. We didn't know them well; only to pass the time of day." A pity; had they been better neighbours, they might have averted a tragedy.

"So Mr. Baxter stayed on next door?" he said after a moment.

"That's right, but he wasn't often there. Went out first thing and came back late at night."

"Where did he work, do you know?"

"Something to do with the post office, I believe."

"Did anyone else ever go to the house? Friends, relatives?"

"Not that we noticed."

"And when was the last time you saw him?"

Grogan thought for a moment. "Sunday. He was cutting his back lawn."

"You didn't see or hear anything last night or early this morning?"

They shook their heads. Then Grogan said suddenly, "Just a minute. Where, exactly, was he murdered?"

"In his back garden, sir."

Mrs. Grogan stared at him with widening eyes. *Just the other side of our fence?*"

"Steady, Beth," said Grogan automatically. Then, "How? Do you know?"

"He appears to have been strangled."

There was a pause while both Grogans reflected on the uncomfortable proximity of this unnatural death. Then Grogan cleared his throat. "There'll be plenty who'll think he got his just deserts. I'm not sure I wouldn't agree with them."

Which was just as Webb had feared. But wife-beater or not, in the law's eyes Baxter had the same rights as anyone else.

He stood up, putting his cup and saucer on the table. "Thank you both for your help. If it's convenient, I'll send someone round later this morning to take your statement. One last thing: was Baxter friendly with anyone in the Close?"

"Not that we know of."

At least, Webb thought as he walked down the drive, the

job of telling the relatives wouldn't be as difficult as usual. They'd probably felt like topping him themselves. Come to think of it, they might even have done so.

It was mid afternoon before the SOCOs had finished with the house and Webb was able to get inside. As the men were packing away their equipment, he walked slowly from room to room, Jackson at his side. The house was identical in layout to its next-door neighbour, but there the resemblance ended. While the Grogans' little nest had been neat and well cared for, this was shabby, with holes in the hall carpet and peeling paintwork. It smelt stale and, despite the dirty dishes piled in the sink, had an unlived-in air.

There were three bedrooms, but the two smaller ones had been stripped, leaving only bare mattresses on the narrow beds. The children's rooms, no doubt. In the bathroom, the single towel was dirty and a black rim lined the bath.

Dick Hodges put his head round the door. "OK, Dave, it's all yours."

"Thanks. Anything of interest in his pockets?"

"Just the usual: house and car keys, wallet with about twenty quid, credit cards all intact. So unless Chummie was disturbed, robbery seems out."

"Not much to go on."

"No. What's more, the ligature was removed, so we can't even check the knot. Still, I have got something to show you. Take a look at this—it was in the waste-paper basket." He handed Webb a plastic exhibit bag containing a note. It was written in a beautiful copperplate, in green ink.

"You have been found guilty of crimes against humanity," he read. "The death sentence will be carried out in eight days. Signed: THE APRIL RAINERS."

"Good God!" Webb said. "Have you got the envelope?"

"Yep. Same writing, postmarked London W1, 27 September."

Webb whistled. "Which is now nine days ago."

Hodges grimaced. "Don't pin your hopes on that—it's one of dozens. The waste-basket was bulging with them. I've seen some hate-mail in my day, but these take the biscuit. What the hell had he done—chopped up his grandma and fed her to the dog?"

"Driven his wife to suicide, it seems, which is enough to be going on with."

"Well, you'll have no shortage of suspects, mate, if you can trace that lot. As I said, the basket was overflowing. Lucky for us he was an untidy bugger and hadn't emptied it."

"Trouble is, Dick, anonymous letter-writers seldom put their threats into effect. Just writing all that stuff gets it off their chests." He frowned, reading the note again. "This one's hardly run-of-the-mill, though. Who the hell are the April Rainers?"

"Search me." Hodges held out his hand and Webb gave him back the packet. "I'll have them all copied and on your desk by the morning."

"Think there's anything in it, guv?" Jackson asked, when they were alone. "Bit of a coincidence, yesterday being eight days after it was written, and he *did* die, like it said."

"It'll have to be looked into, along with everything else. Did you have any luck tracing the sister?"

"Not so far. Don's gone to the shop where Mrs. Baxter worked. She might have had a friend there who'd know."

"Talking of work colleagues, we'll get on to Baxter's. If he'd no friends socially, he might be pally with his workmates. Might even have spent last evening with them. It's a long shot, but worth a try."

The try paid off. In the sorting office at the main post office, they found a man called Taylor who'd spent the previous evening in Baxter's company.

"Ill, is he?" he greeted them. "He's not turned up for work today."

"Did he seem ill when he left you?"

"Didn't say so, but then he doesn't volunteer much, old Ted."

"Had he got his car with him?"

"Ah, so that's it! Over the limit! Well, he can't say we didn't warn him, but you can never reason with Ted. If we try to get him to come with us, he just gets aggressive. Says he's never had an accident yet and doesn't intend to start now." The smile faded from Taylor's face. "He *hasn't* had one, has he?"

"In a manner of speaking," said Webb. "Where did you spend the evening?"

"At the Magpie, out at Chedbury. We play darts every Wednesday."

"What time did you leave?"

"Soon after eleven, I suppose. We walked out to the carpark together."

"And what was the last you saw of him?"

The man shifted uncomfortably. "Look, what is this? What are you getting at?"

"Did you actually see him get into his car?"

"Yes, he was parked next to me."

"So you drove home yourself, sir?" Webb inquired with a straight face.

Taylor flushed. "I watch what I'm drinking. The wife's drummed it into me often enough."

"To come back to Mr. Baxter: he got in his car and drove off?"

"Yes, of course."

"By himself?"

Taylor frowned. "Yes."

"Did you see anyone hanging around? Anyone who might have followed him?"

"No," Taylor said deliberately, "I did not. Now will you for pity's sake tell me what all this is about?"

"I'm sorry to say Mr. Baxter was found dead this morning."

"What?" The man came to his feet. "But—but how? Did he crash the car?"

"No, he appears to have been strangled. In his back garden."

Taylor sat down suddenly. "When did it happen?" he asked after a moment.

"Most likely when he got home after leaving you."

"Poor sod. Poor bloody sod. He'd the devil's own luck." He looked up at Webb. "You heard about his wife?"

"Yes, I heard."

"She was a constant worry to him, always threatening to do away with herself. He never thought she meant it, though."

"Perhaps she wouldn't have, if he hadn't knocked her about," Webb said expressionlessly.

"It didn't mean nothing, it was just the way the drink took him. A lot of men are like that."

"More's the pity. I believe there's a sister. Any idea where she lives?"

"In Ashmartin. She took the kids when Linda died. Ted's been over several times, but they'd never let him see them alone."

"Do you happen to know her name?"

"Yeah—hang on. It was the boy's birthday last week, and Ted brought the card in. Care of—Sanderson, 97 Sheraton Road." He gave a shaky smile. "It gets to be a habit in this job, memorizing names and addresses."

"One final question, Mr. Taylor. Can you think of anyone who might have had it in for him?"

"Not to the extent of killing him, no."

"Well, thanks for your help. Sorry to have been the bearer of bad news."

"And now," he said to Jackson, as they came out onto the street, "since I want to break the news to the sister myself, we'd better get over to Ashmartin." He glanced at Jackson with a smile. "But before you start panicking, we'll pop into the canteen for a cuppa first. OK?"

"OK, guv. Now that you mention it, I am feeling a bit peckish."

"I thought you might be," said Webb. Letting the sergeant take the wheel, he settled back in his seat with a sigh. The day had started early, and it looked like going on for a long time yet. He hoped that by the end of it, they'd have something definite to work on.

2

THAT EVENING, two headlines vied for prominence in the Broadshire *Evening News.* One read: MAN FOUND MURDERED IN RANKIN CLOSE, and the other: COMPOSER RETURNS TO SHILLINGHAM.

Mark Templeton closed the front door behind him and stooped to pick up the paper, his eyes scanning the front page. Barely glancing at the murder report, his attention focused on the other lead story. So there it was, in black and white. No more disappointments, delays, frantic phone calls. She was *here*—Felicity Harwood in person—and in a couple of hours he might even be meeting her.

He walked through to the living-room, his eyes skipping down the column: "World-famous composer and violinist . . . home of her brother, Sir Julian Harwood . . . Ashbourne School for Girls."

But his mind was racing ahead of the words, and with a gesture of impatience he dropped the paper on a chair. He'd read it later; at the moment he was too restless to concentrate, even on that.

Walking to the window, he stood staring out at the lumpy, uneven ground that he euphemistically thought of as "the garden." For as long as he could remember, Felicity Harwood's music had enthralled him. As a boy, his interest had stemmed from the fact that she was born in Shillingham, but as his musical knowledge developed, he came to appreciate her true greatness. For not only was she one of a very small number of women classical composers, she was that rara avis, an equally accomplished performer.

For the last three years, Mark had been music critic for a national newspaper, but his reviews of Miss Harwood's concerts were invariably those which pleased him least. There was an element in her music that defied description, and better critics than himself had failed. Essentially she was a woman of her time, her music a unique blend of past and present, as though she were looking back at the old lyricism from the standpoint of the modern world. Consequently, one movement might be in the Romantic tradition, the next full of the excitement and challenge of the space age. While in less experienced hands the result could seem uneven, in hers it was uniquely effective, evoking conflicting sensations of reassurance and stimulation.

He sighed, glancing at the record cabinets which held boxed collections of her works. Almost every recording she had made was there, as well as performances of her music recorded by other wellknown soloists.

It occurred to him that he must be one of the foremost authorities in the country on Felicity Harwood. For years, he'd read everything that was written about her, travelled whenever he could to her concerts, and written his inadequate critiques. It was through this close following of her schedule that he'd learned, in advance of most people, that she planned to give the world première of her new concerto in her home town, with her brother, resident conductor of the Shillingham Philharmonic, on the podium.

It was then he had had his inspirational idea. Since she was to be in Shillingham, might she be persuaded to give a concert at the school—which, as a girl, she had attended, and which had recently launched an appeal to build a new music wing?

Mark smiled reminiscently, remembering Gwen's initial reaction. "But we *couldn't,* Mark! Whatever would she think?"

"There's no harm in asking. She might like the thought of playing at her alma mater."

"But who'd accompany her? We couldn't afford—"

"The school orchestra," he'd said promptly. "They're jolly good, you know."

"But you couldn't expect a world-famous—"

"My dear aunt!" He only called her that when he was exasperated with her, and Gwen, recognizing that, had smiled. "If you don't invite her, you'll never know, will you? And after the initial approach, which would have to come from you as headmistress, I'd see to all the arrangements. If she turns us down, fair enough, but at least we'll have tried."

Watching her face, he had seen she was being won over, and switched to a more oblique approach. "In the meantime, we'd better apply for our concert tickets. It'll be heavily over-subscribed, which, of course, will mean a lot of disappointment. People would leap at another chance to hear her, and doubtless pay well for the privilege."

It hadn't been easy, though, he reflected now, staring out at the little enclosed plot of land. Naively, he'd expected to deal with Miss Harwood herself, hoping to appeal to her affection for her old school. In fact, all his letters were answered by one H. C. Matthews. Secretary? Agent? Manager? No title followed the name. Mark had only discovered she was a woman a month ago, when, in desperation over another hitch, he'd resorted to the telephone. And pretty formidable she'd sounded, too: the dragon at the gate. No doubt she would also be at the reception this evening.

Still, it had all been worth it. The school concert was scheduled for Wednesday, three days before the public one, and it too had a waiting-list for cancellations. The Music-Wing Appeal was well and truly launched.

The clock on the mantelpiece chimed six, recalling him to his surroundings, and, abandoning his musings, he hurried upstairs to prepare for the evening ahead.

When Mark arrived at the Arts Centre, the reception room was already packed. He shook hands with the mayor and mayoress, the director and various other dignitaries and then, taking a glass of champagne from the tray offered him, moved off in search of someone he knew.

Almost immediately he caught sight of his aunt with Hannah James, her deputy, and made his way over to join them.

"Good evening, ladies," he said easily. "You're looking very glamorous this evening." Gwen, tall, gauche, more like an overgrown schoolgirl than a headmistress, was indeed looking her best. She wore a dark red dress which complemented the flush on her cheeks and added depth to her diffident brown eyes. She'd made an effort, too, with her hair, but as usual, curling tendrils had escaped the severity of their French pleat, to lie softly against her neck. Yet, as Mark himself knew, her gentle appearance was deceptive. His aunt had an iron will, and one baulked her at one's peril. Even his mother, ten years Gwen's senior, had been known to quail before her.

Hannah James, on the other hand, was more conventionally attractive, with her thick, honey-coloured hair, wide brow and clear grey eyes. It was surprising she'd never married, Mark thought; staff-room gossip hinted there was someone in her life, but though wild guesses were put forward, no hard facts had emerged.

"Has Miss Harwood arrived?" he asked, scanning the dense crowd about him.

"I haven't seen her; perhaps she's being shielded from the crush."

"But damn it, she's the one we've all come to see!"

"No doubt she'll appear on the stage in due course and make a pretty speech."

Mark held down his irritation and turned to greet three members of the music staff and a couple of school governors, who had joined their group. This wasn't at all what he'd expected. Still, he'd be meeting Miss Harwood at the school,

so there was no point in letting his frustration spoil the evening. He emptied his glass and looked round for a waiter.
"Anyone else like a refill?" he asked.

"Would anyone notice if I slipped my shoes off?" Cynthia
Jessel murmured to her husband. "They're not meant for
standing around in."

"Surely that's just what they *are* meant for."

"Move over to the wall with me, James. Then I won't be so
conspicuous."

"Dear heart, you're never less than conspicuous."

She glanced up at him but his eyes were circling the room.
As she'd suspected, the compliment had been perfunctory.
Still, the ability to say the right thing at the right time had
served him well, and materially at least she had no cause for
complaint. Emotionally was a different matter. His continual
egotism, his conviction that he was always one step ahead of
the next man, could be very wearing.

"Where is this bloody woman, anyway?" he added, too
loudly for his wife's comfort. "It's seven-thirty, and there
hasn't been sight nor sound of her. I've better things to do
with my time than hang around here all evening."

"For instance?" she challenged him, stepping out of her
shoes.

"What?" His eyes came back to her as she dropped several
inches in height.

"What better things have you to do? Prop up the bar in the
golf club? You're drinking here, and what's more, it's free."

"I've some reports to read before tomorrow, and I must
phone Peabody about the Broadshire *Life* theatre feature."

Cynthia sighed. "I do wish you'd go more gently. It's all
causing a lot of resentment."

"My dear girl, if I'd worried about that, I'd never have got
anywhere."

"But at least take back the editor. She built it up, got it on
a firm footing again, and—"

"Cynthia: do I interfere with your running of the house? Then kindly let me conduct my own affairs. Ah, there are the Conways. I thought they'd be here. Douglas! Hello there!" And, leaving her shoeless against the wall, he pushed his way through the throng to join his friends.

"Ladies and gentlemen!"

About time! thought Mark.

"Could I have your attention, please?" A perspiring little man had appeared on the platform and was speaking into a microphone. Gradually the roar of conversation abated, rustled into silence.

"I know I speak for all of you when I say how privileged we are to have Miss Harwood with us this evening. May I take this opportunity of welcoming her back to Shillingham, and thanking her most sincerely for choosing to give the first performance of her new work in this very building. It is an honour Shillingham will never forget. Ladies and gentlemen, Miss Felicity Harwood."

A slight figure walked slowly onto the stage to the accompaniment of thunderous applause and stood for several moments, smiling and looking down into the hall. Mark, his irritation forgotten, clapped with a lifetime's enthusiasm while he absorbed every detail of her appearance. As always, he was struck by how small she looked alone on the stage, and the deep blue gown accentuated the pallor of her skin and the silver-blond hair, giving an overall air of fragility. And yet again, he marvelled that from that small and delicate frame had come some of the most powerful music of the century.

As the applause continued, she bowed deeply, first to the centre, then to left and right. Finally, she raised her hands, and only then did the clapping fade away.

"Ladies and gentlemen, thank you. I can't tell you how much pleasure it gives me to be back in Shillingham. It holds a very special place in my heart. Thank you all so much for all your support and good wishes."

A small girl climbed carefully up the steps to the stage and presented her with a bouquet of roses and a well-rehearsed curtsey. Another crescendo of applause and the stage was empty.

"I suppose that's it, then," Gwen said, rubbing her tingling palms.

Mark, about to reply, became aware of a breath of heady scent, and turned as a girl brushed past him to touch Gwen's arm. "Excuse me, you are Miss Rutherford? I'm Camilla Harwood. My aunt has asked if you and your party would care to join her in the anteroom."

"We'd be delighted. Thank you."

Mark's spirits soared as, with the others, he followed the girl through one of the exits into a much smaller room. The reception party they'd met earlier were standing by a table laid with plates of canapés and vol-au-vents. Felicity Harwood detached herself from the group and came towards them.

"Miss Rutherford—I'm delighted to meet you. May I introduce my brother and his wife? And my friend, Miss Matthews."

Gwen in turn, more hair escaping in her agitation, introduced her own party. "It was Mr. Templeton's idea to write to you," she added. "I felt it was presumptuous, but he insisted I at least try."

Miss Harwood turned to Mark, who said with a smile, "On the basis that faint heart never won fair lady!"

"Charmingly put. I should have been most upset *not* to be asked, when it's to benefit the school. It's also a chance to thank you personally for your kind reception of my work. You *are* the Mark Templeton who writes those reviews?"

"I am, yes."

"And very sensitively, too. If I may say so without sounding patronizing, you show great feeling for the music."

He murmured his thanks, and, sensing his embarrassment,

she smiled and moved on to the school governors. Mark watched her, consciously trying to store up every detail of this evening for the years ahead. Close to, he noted, she looked more her age than she appeared on the concert platform. There were fine lines round eyes and mouth, and veins stood out in her hands. Her hair, too, which he'd thought of as blond, was more silver than fair.

Suddenly conscious of being watched in his turn, Mark glanced to his left to meet the amused gaze of the girl who had brought them here, and experienced a jolt of belated awareness. Only the presence of Felicity Harwood could have blinded him to the attractions of her niece.

He smiled. "Was I in moonstruck-calf mode? I'm sorry, but she's been my idol for as long as I can remember."

"Oh, mine too. I've swanked about her all my life."

"Are you a musician?"

She shook her head. "We've enough of them in the family. Mother and I are the practical ones."

"So what do you do?"

"I work in television. You won't have heard of me; it's mostly afternoon programmes. Interesting, though. I love it."

"Here, or in London?"

"Both. At the moment I'm working at the Shillingham studios, so I'm taking advantage of a bit of home comfort. What do you do, apart from review concerts?"

"Oh, that's only a fringe activity. For my bread and butter, I teach the violin."

"At Miss Rutherford's school?"

"Most of the time. I visit a couple of others too, and have some private pupils."

"Good evening, Mr. Templeton," said a crisp voice at his elbow, and, cursing the interruption, Mark turned to face Miss Matthews. "It's not often I meet someone as stubborn as I am."

Camilla laughed. "Coming from Hattie, that's a compliment!"

"Well, I did my best to discourage him; I felt—and I still do—that two concerts within a week is too much, but his persistence wore me down. And of course, when I mentioned it to Felicity, the battle was lost. She doesn't appreciate how much a performance takes out of her."

"She thrives on it," said Camilla stoutly, "just as Daddy does."

So this was the dragon custodian—a more accurate description than he'd guessed. Hattie Matthews was a plain woman; her nondescript hair was uncompromisingly clipped behind her ears, her skin was coarse, and her hips large. Definitely absent when the good looks were handed out. Mark wondered what could have persuaded anyone as ethereal and talented as Felicity Harwood to put herself and her career in this woman's hands.

"She's not as young as she was," she was saying firmly, "and there's the American tour next month. This visit was supposed to be a rest, but it's being whittled away all the time. Not only are there the two concerts, but the week after, she has to fly to Edinburgh to receive the Freedom of the City."

The director had approached, and was hovering beside them. "Sorry to interrupt," he said as they turned to him, "but Miss Harwood's ready to go into the hall now. Only for a few minutes," he added quickly, as Miss Matthews drew breath to protest, "but she doesn't want to disappoint the crowd."

Felicity Harwood was moving towards the door with her brother and sister-in-law, and Mark saw Sir Julian beckon his daughter to join them. He said quickly, "You're coming to the school concert?"

"Of course," Camilla replied. "See you then, I hope." He watched her go through the doorway to the hall, her slim, lithe figure in striking contrast to Hattie Matthews's large and clumsy one. And he found himself hoping that her current TV project would keep her in Shillingham for some time.

Gwen was beside him. "Isn't she absolutely charming?"

"Absolutely!"

"And how gratifying that she reads your reviews!"

Mark murmured a reply, but he was disconcerted. His automatic response had referred not to Felicity Harwood but to her niece, and the realization that, however temporarily, she had distracted him from the long-dreamed-of meeting with the composer kept him in thoughtful mood for the rest of the evening.

It was midnight by the time Webb got back to his flat. Wearily he hung his jacket on the hook and extracted from its pocket the evening paper he'd bought earlier. Then he went into the kitchen, dropping it on the table while he poured himself a drink. He'd had nothing to eat since the snatched sandwich in the canteen with Jackson. The insistence of Ken's stomach on regular sustenance had doubtless saved them both from ulcers over the years. He knew it would be sensible to eat now, but he was past hunger and too tired to bother. Stifling a yawn, he pulled out the wooden chair and sat down, glass in hand, to review the day.

The visit to Ashmartin had proved a trying one. Mrs. Sanderson, though shocked by the news of her brother-in-law's death, had wasted no time on expressions of regret.

"Well, he had it coming to him," she said. "He deserved putting down, a brute like that."

"I realize it's painful for you to speak about your sister, but we'd be grateful for some details of what happened."

Her eyes had filled at once. "I don't see what this has to do with Linda. It's just a pity he wasn't killed sooner, then she needn't have died."

"Was their marriage always unhappy?"

"He always drank, if that's what you mean, but I don't think he was violent in the early days. She never said anything, but then we had to force it out of her, even at the end. I don't think she'd ever have told us, if we hadn't called round and found her covered in bruises. Too loyal by half, she was." Mrs. Sanderson broke off to wipe her eyes with her handkerchief.

"It was you and your husband who persuaded her to report him?"

She nodded. "But once she had, she was so relieved. She thought it was all over, you see. 'Oh Norma,' she said, 'it'll be so wonderful, not to have to listen for him coming home every night, wondering what state he'll be in. I don't think I could have taken it much longer.' And after all that, those— those flaming do-gooders let him go! 'We're sure you've learned your lesson, Mr. Baxter,' " she mimicked savagely. "They mightn't have been so ready to turn the other cheek, if it was their cheek he was hitting." And she'd buried her face in her handkerchief and sobbed bitterly.

"What happened next?" Webb asked after a moment.

Mrs. Sanderson sniffed and mopped at her eyes. "Well, we did our best to get her to come back with us, but she said she couldn't, because of school—the new term was just about to start. But something must have happened later, because the next morning she rang up in a terrible state. 'Norma,' she said, 'I want you to promise me something. If anything happens to me, will you and Jim take the children?'

"Well, that really frightened me. I thought Ted was threatening to kill her or something, but I couldn't get any sense out of her. All she kept saying was 'Promise me! Promise!' So of course I did, but when I tried to get her to tell me what was wrong, she hung up. So I rang Jim at the office. He came home to collect me and we drove straight over to Shillingham, but by the time we got there, it was too late. She must have taken the pills before she phoned me. There was a note saying she was sorry—*she* was sorry!—and that the children were at a friend's house."

"How did her husband react to her death?"

"Well, he was very shocked, I must admit. Broke down and cried like a child, but I'd no sympathy with him. I told him straight it was him that drove her to it. So we packed up the children's things and brought them straight back here."

"How old are they?"

"Seven and nine."

"Are they coping all right?"

She shrugged. "It's hard to say. But we've always been close to them—comes from not having any of our own."

"And their father's been over to see them?"

"A couple of times, yes, but Jim always stayed in the room with them. I wouldn't see Ted—I went upstairs till he'd left the house."

As tactfully as he could, Webb had inquired how she and her husband had spent the previous evening, and was told they'd had friends in for whist.

"It may seem heartless, Chief Inspector, but Jim insisted we keep up the regular foursome. Said it would take my mind off things."

"Very sensible. Mrs. Sanderson, has Mr. Baxter any other relatives apart from yourselves?"

"Only a brother out in Australia. His parents died years ago."

"Then I'm afraid we must ask either you or your husband to identify him."

She blanched, clutching her throat. "Oh, Jim'll have to. I couldn't—it would turn my stomach."

Fortunately it was at this point that her husband returned from work, and the solemn little cortege had immediately set out for Shillingham. Back at his desk, Webb found a report awaiting him of a break-in the previous evening in Rankin Road. With a bit of luck, there might be a tie-in.

So there it was, he thought, draining his glass. Though the Sandersons must have had as strong a motive as anyone for despatching Baxter, their alibi was confirmed, and the investigation advanced only by elimination.

He pulled the evening paper towards him, grimacing at the headline. Bill Hardy had done his homework, he reflected, reading the report. It was all there—Baxter's appearance in court, his subsequent return home and his wife's suicide.

"Crimes against humanity," he thought suddenly. The April Rainers, whoever they were, had been right on that. Had they also, unlike most anonymous letter-writers, carried out their "death sentence"? Only time would tell.

He stood up, stretching and running a hand through his hair, too tired to concentrate any more. He was turning from the table when his eyes fell on the other main headline—COMPOSER RETURNS TO SHILLINGHAM. This would be the woman Hannah'd been telling him about. Well, he hadn't a cat in hell's chance of getting to the concert now, with a murder on his hands.

Switching off the light, he went to run himself a bath.

3

THERE WAS ANOTHER PARAGRAPH in that evening's paper which, since it was the end of a long-running story, did not merit a place on the front page. It was, however, of immense significance to several people in the county, and to none more than the Fenshawes.

BROADSHIRE LIFE IMAGE TO CHANGE, it read. And, underneath: "After his successful bid for Broadshire *Life,* Mr. James Jessel has lost no time in restructuring both the glossy magazine and its premises. It has been confirmed that former editor Gaby Fenshawe, who was credited with saving the prestigious publication from liquidation three years ago and trebling its circulation, has been replaced following the takeover.

" 'We want a new image,' Mr. Jessel told our reporter, 'and I have every confidence that the appointment of Colin Campbell as editor is the first step towards achieving this.' "

Nat Fenshawe was re-reading the report when his wife came into the kitchen the next morning.

"Throw it out, Nat," she said philosophically. "It's yesterday's paper and yesterday's news. Today there'll be something new to read about and I'll be forgotten."

"I don't know how you can be so calm about it," he said bitterly, watching her toss the paper in the bin. "At least take the bastard to a tribunal. Everyone knows it was unfair dismissal and you'd get plenty of backing."

"No doubt, but I've too much pride to go whingeing to

court. And I don't want to stay on anyway. I can't stand the man—wouldn't be able to keep a civil tongue in my head."

"You'd at least get financial compensation."

She laughed. "Oh, Nat, I'm not on the scrapheap yet! I'll find another job without too much difficulty. Probably a better one. I've made a name for myself now."

He put an arm round her and pulled her fiercely against him. "Gaby love, you needn't pretend with me. When I think of the time and energy you put into that magazine, and the nights you sat up slaving over it, I could strangle the bastard. And the supreme irony, of course, is that if you *hadn't* pulled it back from the brink, engaged the best writers and so on, Jessel wouldn't have wanted to buy it anyway."

"You're taking it harder than I am," Gaby said with a smile. She reached up to give him a quick kiss, and moved away to fill the kettle. She knew Nat wasn't deceived by her flippancy, but she was reluctant to let even him see the depth of her hurt. If only the old boys had had enough faith in her, she thought for the hundredth time; given her another six months. Then they'd have realized the crisis was over and the magazine would survive. But they were past it, bless them, Mr. Henry well into his seventies and Mr. Edward turned eighty, for heaven's sake. The Stratton brothers, who *were* Broadshire *Life.*

But Jessel Enterprises were big business, and they'd made a very tempting offer. The old men had dithered, and she knew how their minds must have worked. Suppose Gaby ran out of steam? Safer for all concerned if she had solid financial backing. So, sadly, but feeling they were doing the best for their staff—most of whom regarded them as joint grandfathers—the two old men had stepped down, and now a stranger sat in their office. A stranger who had sidestepped their stipulations on redundancies, and was in the process of altering the entire nature of the magazine.

"At least I'm still alive," she said aloud. Terence Denbigh

of the "Denbigh's Diary" column had collapsed and died on learning of his dismissal.

Nat slammed his hand on the table, and Gaby regretted her comment. He was inflamed enough against Jessel, without reminding him of the loss of a friend; the elderly widower had frequently joined them for supper, amusing them with his gently ironic view of the world.

"There comes a point," Nat said viciously, "when that man has to be stopped from trampling people underfoot, and it has now been reached. Enough is enough."

Gaby said placatingly, "Look, love, forget it. There's nothing you can do."

"On the contrary, there is. Mr. James Bloody Jessel is going to get his come-uppance, and I shall have great pleasure in administering it. In fact, it's already under way."

Cynthia Jessel looked up from her own mail at her husband's exclamation. "What is it?"

"Another of those stupid anonymous letters."

"I told you you're making a lot of enemies."

"And I told you that if I were to let my life be ruled by sentiment, I might as well throw in the sponge. You don't make money by being soft-hearted."

She eyed the screwed-up ball of paper. "What does it say?"

"A lot of mumbo-jumbo, but the basic message is death and disaster. Signed, if you please, by 'The April Rainers.' "

"Who are they?"

"Search me. A bunch of religious maniacs, most likely."

"You should hand it to the police."

He snorted. "And what can they do?" He glanced at the envelope. "It was posted in London—a needle in a haystack. Forget it; I intend to." He pushed back his chair. "I must be going; I've a meeting with Campbell at nine."

"James, are you sure you weren't over-hasty about the Fenshawe girl? With her flair she'd be an asset, and keeping her on would avoid some of the unpleasantness. You're already blamed for the death of the diarist."

"Poppycock. You know I can't work with women at that level—they're too temperamental. In any case, I didn't care for her—she seemed to think *she* owned the magazine. There'd have been a personality clash before long; better simply to forestall it."

It would take a saint *not* to clash with James, Cynthia thought. It wasn't pleasant being married to someone as disliked as he was, but she'd learned to live with it. Broodingly, she looked across at him, at the thick, curly hair, the broad shoulders, the rather loose mouth. Well, if he wanted to make still more enemies, it was no skin off her nose.

"So just drop it, will you. Surprisingly enough, I do know what I'm doing." He left the room, and a moment later the front door closed behind him.

Cynthia reached across, retrieved the ball of paper and smoothed it out on the table. Subconsciously, she associated anonymous letters with phrases cut from newspapers, or illiterate scrawl. This was neither; it was printed in copperplate letters in a striking green ink, which somehow lent importance to its contents. It read: "You are found guilty of evil deeds which assault and hurt the soul. The death sentence will be carried out in eight days. Signed: THE APRIL RAINERS."

Cynthia shivered involuntarily. James was right, it had a quasi-religious tone. Weren't some of the words from the Prayer Book? At school, she'd been required to learn and recite each week's collect, and they'd lain dormant in her brain for thirty years. Now, she dredged the appropriate phrases to the surface: ". . . that we might be defended from all adversities which may happen to the body, and from all evil"—thoughts, surely, not deeds— "which may assault and hurt the soul." Which, if it was a deliberate misquotation, was interesting. Evil thoughts might be considered to hurt one's own soul; evil deeds, primarily someone else's.

She slewed the envelope round. The postmark was the previous day, which reduced the time-limit to a week. Well, if James wasn't going to bother about it, she didn't see why she should, though she still thought he ought to tell the police.

Picking up both note and envelope, she crumpled them in her hand and dropped them into the waste-paper basket. Then, putting the episode out of her mind, she turned her attention to the day ahead.

Webb sat at his desk, tapping his pen as he reviewed the position. Six teams of detectives had left Carrington Street police station an hour earlier, and in his mind he went over the Actions they'd been assigned.

1. Ask householders in Rankin Road if any unfamiliar cars had been parked there on Wednesday evening. (He was still hopeful of a link with the break-in.)

2. Inquire whether any neighbours saw or heard Baxter return home. If so, check timing in case he stopped on the way, perhaps to pick up his killer.

3. Interview the landlord of the Magpie at Chedbury, and see if any strangers were in the pub that night. If so, did they speak to Ted Baxter?

4. Interview Baxter's colleagues at the post office, including Ron Taylor. Names needed of group who played darts with Baxter.

5. Follow up the latter and question them.

6. Go through victim's diary and address book and follow up entries.

7. Revisit Mrs. Baxter's place of work and interview any close colleagues.

He sighed, glancing again at the post mortem report. It wasn't much help; Stapleton wouldn't commit himself on the missing ligature, merely stating it was "likely to have been something in the nature of a nylon stocking."

"Problems, Dave?"

Webb looked across at Alan Crombie, now returned from his prolonged course at Bramshill. "You name 'em, I've got 'em."

"Including a surfeit of suspects?"

"Yep, all anonymous, which doesn't help a lot. Most of the letters are pretty run-of-the-mill, but there was one that stood out. For the hell of it, I've had it teleprinted and circulated, but with instructions not to divulge it to the press."

His phone rang and he reached for it.

"DCI Webb? DI Francis, sir, Snow Hill. I've just seen your teleprint on the anonymous letter. A couple of years ago, a note signed 'The April Rainers' came to light here during a murder investigation."

Giving Crombie the "thumbs up," Webb leant forward. "Yes, Inspector?"

"Unfortunately we never traced it and the case is still open."

"Great."

"The note was printed in green copperplate, just like yours. Even more significantly, it, too, gave the victim eight days to live, and he was killed on the appointed day."

"Who was the victim?"

"A nasty piece of work, sir, Thomas Raymond by name. He'd a fine racket going: sold franchises for health-food shops, and the agreements all stipulated—in small print—that the buyers could only get their supplies from named sources. Naturally, he owned all said sources himself, and sold to them at extortionate prices. Four or five couples were caught —put their savings into buying the franchise, then went bust and no recompense."

"Um. To come back to the note; do you remember the exact words?"

"I've got it here, sir. I looked it out before phoning. It says, 'In payment for the anguish and hardship you've caused, your life will be terminated in eight days.' And it's signed 'The April Rainers.' "

"What was the MO?"

"Asphyxiation, but we're not sure with what; the ligature had been removed."

"That," said Webb slowly, "is very interesting. Very interesting indeed. And you'd no idea who was behind it?"

"Oh, we had our suspicions—among them, an oddball group who were crusading to reintroduce moral values. They'd certainly been in touch with Raymond, but we weren't able to tie them in with his murder."

"Were they based in your area?"

"Yes, but they travel round the country on what they call 'missions.' They could be in your part of the world. I'll check if you like."

"Please. Did the name 'April Rainers' appear in the press?"

"No, sir. We held it back."

"Good. Well, I'll send a couple of my men over to look into it. I'd be grateful for any assistance you can give them."

"Of course, sir."

"One last thing. Where was your note posted?"

"W1. One of the busiest areas, naturally—Oxford Street, and round there. No hope of tracing it back."

"I gather Chummie has struck before," Crombie said, as Webb replaced the phone.

"It looks like it. Snow Hill had a similar note two years ago —green ink, eight-day deadline, if you'll pardon the pun. And it wasn't publicized at the time, which rules out the copy-cat factor. Though if the notes *are* connected, it's a long time between crimes."

"Unless there have been others which haven't come to light."

"Thanks, Alan, that makes me feel a lot better. Get over to the Smoke, will you, and look into it? The usual routine— draw out the file, interrogate the officers who were in charge, etc. Take young Marshbanks with you and stay overnight if necessary, but dig deep. We need all the help we can get on this one."

The school orchestra were rehearsing, as they had for months, the *William Tell* Overture they would perform at next week's concert. Nerves were on edge, and Tim Ladbury had taken them through it three times already. To Mark, seated at the back of the Queen's Hall, it sounded pretty good, all things considered.

He was humming the theme under his breath when a fourth-former came and tapped him on the shoulder. "Excuse me, Mr. Templeton, Miss Hanson said to tell you you're wanted on the phone."

Mark followed her out of the hall, the lovely music ringing in his ears, and made his way to the office. The school secretary looked up with a smile.

"Lady Harwood, no less!" she said softly, nodding to the phone. "Let's hope your soloist hasn't changed her mind!"

Mark lifted the receiver. "Hello?"

"Good afternoon, Mr. Templeton; this is Elizabeth Harwood. We met briefly at the reception."

She waited for his murmur of assent.

"My sister-in-law tells me she had time for only a few words with you last night, and there are certain points that she'd like to discuss. We were wondering if it would be convenient for you to come and have lunch with us tomorrow?"

"Yes—yes, of course. Thank you—I'd be delighted."

"About twelve-thirty, then? You know where we live? It's not far from the school—Hampton Rise. Fauconberg House, on the right-hand side."

"I'll find it. Thank you very much, Lady Harwood."

Camilla'd be there, too, he thought, his spirits rising. What a bit of luck, after all, that he hadn't seen more of Felicity Harwood last evening.

It was after ten by the time Webb got home, and he'd only just taken off his mac when the doorbell rang. He opened the door to find Hannah there, holding a large bowl of mushrooms.

"They were on special offer at the market," she said. "I couldn't resist them, but there are more than I want, and I thought you might like some."

"They look lovely—thanks."

He led the way into the kitchen, took last night's paper from the table, and lined the top basket of the vegetable rack with it.

"I presume this murder case is yours?" she commented, as she tipped the mushrooms over the black headlines.

" 'Fraid so."

"And you've only just got in, haven't you? I came up half an hour ago."

"At least it's a couple of hours earlier than last night."

"Have you eaten?"

"Nope."

"Like me to rustle up something?"

He grinned. "What would I do without you?"

"Mushroom omelette sound all right?"

"Wonderful, if I'd any eggs, but I ate the last one on Wednesday."

"I've told you before I'd do your shopping when you're on a case—you only have to ask. We can't have police efficiency impaired by malnutrition! Let me know what you need, and I'll get it tomorrow. In the meantime, since I've plenty of eggs, we'll go downstairs."

Hannah's flat, on the floor below, overlooked the back of the house. It was larger and more spacious than Webb's, and as always he entered it with a feeling of pleasure. Something in the cool colours and attractive decor, the comfortable chairs and airy unclutteredness gave him an immediate sense of peace and relaxation.

On a cushion in a corner of the hall lay a small ginger

kitten, which looked up briefly at their entrance, then curled back into sleep. Webb nodded towards it.

"You're not finding that a tie?"

Hannah's recent stint of cat-minding, while involving her in a murder case, had also reawakened her love of cats.*

"Not at all, he's as good as gold. I take him with me to school and he behaves perfectly."

"Like Mary's lamb," said Webb drily. He followed her into the kitchen, sniffing appreciatively at the faint aroma of herbs and spices, overlaid by the scent of the plants flourishing on the window-sill. "I didn't realize how hungry I was," he remarked, hitching himself on a corner of the table and watching her take smooth brown eggs from the fridge.

"In that case, I'll double the quantity." She moved calmly about the kitchen, taking down pans and utensils without seeming to mar the orderliness of the room.

"Have you any suspects yet?" she asked, whisking the eggs.

"Four dozen or so, all anonymous."

She frowned. "Letter-writers? I read about the court case and the wife's death."

"Letter-writers," Webb confirmed. He added casually, "Know anything about the April Rainers?"

"Only that there were eight of them. Why?"

"That's how one of the letters was signed. It's from 'Green Grow the Rushes-O,' isn't it? Any idea of the origin?"

"I know it's very old. While you have your supper, I'll look it up and see what I can find."

The supper tray, consisting of the large, golden omelette, bread and butter and a cup of coffee, was carried through to the sitting-room and put on a low table by the window. The room was still arranged for summer, with the window rather than the fire as the focal point.

"I put off moving things back as long as possible," Hannah

* *Six Proud Walkers*

commented, as Webb seated himself in the apple-green chair. She laid her own coffee-cup on the table and moved to the bookcase, running her fingers along the spines and selecting a large reference-book which she brought back to her chair.

"The song's older than I realized," she remarked a moment later. "It's appeared in Hebrew, French and Spanish, and the first time it was written down in English was in 1625. There are several different versions even in this country, but it's always assumed to have a theological basis."

"The Ten Commandments and the Twelve Apostles, yes. But April Rainers?"

"It'll be a corruption, of course, and actually this verse seems to have caused the most confusion. One version is 'Bold Rainers,' which is assumed to refer to angels, though why eight, I don't know. Another gives 'Bold Rangers' and refers to the eight members of Noah's family in the Ark."

"I can hardly rope them in!"

"If that's no help, you have a choice of 'Eight Commanders' or 'Gabriel Riders.'" She looked up, pushing back her hair. "Doesn't seem much help, does it?"

"Not a lot," said Webb with his mouth full. "It's the number that worries me, though. Do we assume it's a joint letter from eight different people? A gang of some sort?"

"Goodness knows." Hannah rose and replaced the book on the shelf. "Anyway, I hope you'll clear it up quickly, and be free to come to the concerts."

"I don't think I've a hope, love. Certainly not by Wednesday."

"Gwen and I went to the reception last evening, and were invited to the inner sanctum to meet Felicity Harwood. It was quite exciting."

"Just you and Gwen?"

"No, of course not. There was the mayor and—"

"Just you and Gwen from the school?"

She met his eyes and answered steadily. "No, Mark was

there, and Tim Ladbury and a couple of other members of staff and two of the governors."

"Charles Frobisher?"

"Yes, David, Charles Frobisher was one of them." She held his gaze challengingly. It was over a year now since she had rejected Charles's proposal of marriage, but she knew David was still uneasy at their regular professional contact.

"I'm sorry," he said quietly, laying down his empty plate. "It's none of my business."

Hannah watched him as he finished his coffee. Theirs was an odd relationship; it purported to make no demands, but the facts were rather different. When David's ex-wife had returned briefly, Hannah'd been startled by the depth of her hurt, as had he, later, when she'd turned to Charles. Tacitly, they accepted that, while for their own reasons they'd no wish to marry, there was a strong bond between them that neither wanted to break. Occasionally, depending on their different jobs, they might not see each other for weeks— apart, perhaps, from passing on the stairs. There were times when they met as friends, delighting in each other's company but asking nothing more. And there were times when they came together as lovers, seeking and finding in each other a passionate tenderness that was essential to their wellbeing. Only once, when Charles had asked her to marry him, had David said that he loved her, and it had not been referred to again. Hannah was content that it should be so.

He leant back in his chair and smiled across at her. "That should give me enough energy to get back up the stairs; which, regretfully, I must now do. It'll be a heavy day again tomorrow."

He stood up and drew her gently into his arms, his cheek resting on her silky hair. She was his oasis, where he could rest and recharge himself for the ordeals that lay ahead. And if he didn't release her, he thought ruefully, he mightn't get that early night after all. Reluctantly he did so, and Hannah walked with him to the door. Again the kitten looked up sleepily, and Webb was reminded of that other cat that had watched from the garage in Rankin Close.

Hannah paused to scoop up the orange scrap.

"Do you put him out at night?"

"Certainly not. An owl might mistake him for a mouse!"

Webb touched the tiny head with one finger. "What is it you call him?"

"Pekoe, like Orange Pekoe tea. Talking of which, what groceries do you need?"

"If you're sure it's no trouble, I'll drop a list through your door in the morning. Thanks, love. Sleep well." He bent his head and kissed her.

"You'll call for your shopping tomorrow evening?"

"If it's not too late, yes."

As he ran back up the stairs to his flat, Webb's thoughts had already slipped from Hannah to the interpretations of the old rhyme. Noah's Ark, indeed! That was all he needed! he thought, and was grinning as he put his key in the lock.

4

HAMPTON RISE, unlike its near neighbour Hillcrest, where Webb lived, still boasted the large and gracious houses of a bygone age, the 1950s developers having mercifully run out of money before they could demolish them and set up soulless blocks of flats in their place.

Since he had come from home and not the school, Mark arrived by car, to find the gates of Fauconberg House standing open. He turned in and drove down the immaculately gravelled drive to the front door. A uniformed maid admitted him and showed him to the drawing-room, where the family awaited him.

Camilla came forward, dispelling his momentary awkwardness on entering a roomful of eminent and virtually unknown people. His first quick glance had taken in Sir Julian and Lady Harwood, Felicity, Hattie Matthews and an elderly lady who sat with a rug over her knees.

"Come and meet my grandmother," Camilla said, taking his arm.

Mrs. Harwood looked old and frail; veins stood out on her temples and the flesh had fallen away from her cheekbones. But the faded eyes were alert, and she smiled her welcome. "I'm glad to meet you, Mr. Templeton. My daughter tells me you're one of her most ardent admirers!"

"Indeed I am," Mark acknowledged. "I think I've attended all the concerts she's given in the U.K. over the last ten years."

"You deserve a long-service medal!" said Felicity at his side. "I'm so glad you could come; there are a lot of things I want to speak to you about, but they'll keep till after lunch."

The conversation became general, and under cover of it, Mark discreetly studied his hosts. "Fine-honed" was the best description of Sir Julian; he was tall and spare of frame, and his face looked curiously streamlined. Nose, brows and cheeks seemed to have little flesh to cover the underlying bone structure, and his skin was taut and polished. His eyes, like those of his mother and sister, were a keen, pale blue and his fine hair—either fair or grey, it was difficult to tell—thinly covered his scalp from a receding forehead. But despite his intellectual air, his smile had been pleasant and his handshake firm.

His wife, Elizabeth, had what used to be called "breeding." She was of middle height and with a tendency to plumpness; her voice was low and cultured, her brow untroubled, and her soft brown hair sprinkled with grey. She gave the appearance of a woman serenely content in the bosom of her family. After the strains and stresses of his profession, her husband must bless her air of quietude.

Camilla took her colouring from her mother, though her hair was lighter and her eyes deepset like her father's. She had also inherited his oval face and tall, slim figure. Watching her, Mark again found himself attracted by her casual air of independence and the bantering look in her eyes. Here was a girl who knew what she wanted and would, he felt, have little trouble getting it.

At lunch, he was seated between his hostess and Felicity, with Camilla directly opposite. Almost at once, Felicity claimed his attention, and he perforce set himself to answering her virtually nonstop questions—about his family, his career, his ambitions, and his views on the various interpretations of her music.

The rest of the party chatted among themselves, apparently unconcerned by the exclusive conversation in their midst.

Mrs. Harwood was not with them; it seemed she was more comfortable eating in her room with her live-in nurse.

"Is your grandmother not well?" Mark asked Camilla, when Felicity at last paused to give some attention to her plate. He was unsure whether the old lady's frailty was due simply to her age.

It was Felicity who replied. "The doctor gives her six weeks. She thinks I'm here to rest before the American tour, but it's really to spend as much time with her as I can. She might not be here when I get back."

"I'm sorry," Mark said inadequately, but Felicity had already resumed her interrogation. He glanced at Camilla and was disconcerted to note her amusement. She leant forward.

"Dearest aunt, have mercy on our guest! He's hardly eaten a mouthful between answering all your questions!"

"No, really," he protested, "it's perfectly all right."

But Felicity was penitent. "I'm so sorry—I have been monopolizing you. I promise not to say another word till you've finished your meal."

Despite his disclaimer, Mark was glad to join in more general conversation for the rest of the meal. But when they'd finished their coffee and rose to leave the room, Felicity reclaimed him.

"Now for our discussion. We'll go to the music room. It shouldn't take long."

The Harwoods' music room was rather different from his own, but Mark barely had time to take in its decor or the magnificent instruments that filled it. As the door closed behind them, Felicity began without preamble. "You must be wondering why I asked you here."

"To finalize the concert?"

"We covered that in correspondence. There's something else I want to discuss."

She walked to the French windows and stood looking out at the garden. Following her gaze, Mark saw that most of the trees had changed colour. Autumn was here, and soon the grass would be thick with leaves.

Felicity spoke without turning. "You've probably never given it much thought, but in my position, an occupational hazard is being approached by people wanting to write one's biography."

"Yes, I suppose so," Mark agreed uncertainly.

"I've turned down three this year already."

He could think of nothing to add, so kept silent. She hadn't invited him to sit, and he remained standing, looking at her silhouette against the window and, beyond her, the sunlit garden.

She turned back into the room, and as her face was against the light, he couldn't read her expression.

"I was wondering if you'd like to do it," she said.

He stared at her, completely dumbfounded, incapable of any reply.

"I might say the family thinks I'm mad," she went on quickly. "Not out of any disrespect for you, but simply because, as far as we know, you've never done anything of the kind before. Have you?"

Mark could only shake his head.

"But you see, there's an affinity between us. I'm sure I could relax with you, as I couldn't with the others. Even more important, I think you understand my music better than they do, despite all the letters after their names. They're *writers,* you see, and you're a musician. Yet you write about music so beautifully and so—intuitively. And you were saying you never miss my concerts. You must know more about my work than anyone else in your field."

Vaguely, Mark remembered reaching the same conclusion, only two days ago.

"I know it would take time, that's why I was asking about your career. Would you be able to take a sabbatical, do you think? If you had, say, a year off, you could make a really good start and then proceed more slowly. For instance, a lot of my papers are here, scores and so on. You could go through those at your leisure later—that's one of the advantages of your living in Shillingham. Another is that you know my background—you even teach at my old school. Don't you see you're the perfect choice?"

She paused and, when he still did not speak, added, "You'd be able to accompany me on concert tours, and we could continue with interviews any time I'm in London."

She stopped speaking at last, and the silence between them was measured by the steady tick of the clock in the corner. Mark spread his hands helplessly. "I—don't know what to say. It's come so completely out of the blue."

"It would give your career a boost," she remarked shrewdly. "And since I'd be commissioning you, I'd see that the financial arrangements were generous. You wouldn't lose out on your year away from teaching."

He said slowly, "Miss Harwood—"

"Felicity, please."

He made a little gesture with his hand. "Felicity—I can't tell you how honoured I am, but I'm completely overwhelmed. I've never tackled anything remotely like a biography—I wouldn't know where to start."

"At the beginning, perhaps?" she suggested smilingly. "With my childhood, here in this house and at Ashbourne. I kept diaries from the age of ten—they'd be useful."

"There's also the practical side," he went on. "You suggest a sabbatical, and I'd certainly need something of the sort, but it would take a lot of arranging. I visit other schools as well as Ashbourne, and there are my private pupils to consider. I'd have to make arrangements for them, and that can't be done at the drop of a hat. Also, as you'll realize, the school year has just begun."

She walked slowly towards him. "Are you turning me down, Mark?"

"I'm—not sure. Oh, look," he burst out, "of *course* I'd love to do it—be with you while you rehearse, perform—but I don't see how I can. And even if we do find a way, it wouldn't be for some time."

She smiled. "My trouble has always been that when I want something, I want it at once. I was even going to suggest we make a start this week, while I'm in Shillingham."

His programme for the week ahead flashed in front of him: playing Felicity's part at rehearsals on Monday; Tuesday and Thursday visiting other schools, with private lessons in the evenings; and Wednesday the concert itself.

She'd been watching his face. "At least it's not a definite no?"

He smiled ruefully. "Not quite definite."

"Then I've a suggestion. Suppose you make a provisional start? You could tape a few conversations with me, make some local inquiries about my childhood, and see how it goes. Then, if you become hooked, as I hope you will, we can work on more concrete plans. Of course I see, now that I've thought about it, that you can't drop everything at my whim. I promise I won't rush you. Just give it a try and see how it goes. How about that?"

"All right. Sorry to put such a damper on it, but I've a pretty hectic schedule, with just about every working hour accounted for. It's a pity it didn't come up before the long school holidays."

"Indeed it is. Never mind, we should manage a couple of interviews while I'm here. I hope you're free tomorrow?"

Abandoning a proposed day with Jackie, Mark nodded. "I'll bring a tape-recorder," he said. "And it would save time if I left the machine with you afterwards. Then, any time you had a spare moment, you could talk about your early life or anything else that came into your head."

"That's an excellent idea. But for the moment, I've taken up quite enough of your time. Let's rejoin the others."

As they emerged into the hall, Camilla was coming out of the drawing-room. Her glance moved from her aunt's face to Mark's. Neither gave much away.

"Ah, there you are. I wondered if you'd like a tour of the garden?"

"Yes, I should. Thank you."

Felicity said, "Enjoy yourselves, children. I'm going up to sit with Mother for a while. See you at tea."

They walked out of the front door and round the side of the house to the lawns Mark had seen from the music room. Camilla glanced at his set face.

"You look in need of some fresh air!"

"You know what we were talking about?"

"Oh yes. We've heard little else since Thursday evening. My aunt's very impressed with you; she thinks you'd be a worthy chronicler."

"I hadn't the slightest idea what was coming—I thought she wanted to discuss the concert."

"What do you think of the idea?"

"I honestly don't know. But I can't just drop everything. Which is what she seems to want."

Camilla smiled. "That's Felicity all over. She makes up her mind at lightning speed and tries to rush everyone else along with her. Where her music's concerned, she's completely single-minded and, it has to be said, totally self-centred. She told me once that she has to be, in order to force through the interpretations she wants."

Mark's mind was on the proposed biography. "Even if I'd the time, I don't know if I could do it."

"I think you could."

He smiled slightly. "I'm flattered, but you haven't much to go on."

"Enough. You write well—I read your reviews, too. You already know a great deal about her music, and you admire her so much. That's important. So many biographers nowadays seem more interested in writing exposés to make their books sell."

"Well, you can rest assured that if I do take on the job, her reputation will be safe!"

Camilla laughed. "Good. Now, come and see the dahlia bed. It's just at its best."

"For God's sake!" James Jessel was shouting, "I should know whether I've ordered any manure or not! Will you stop saying I must have!"

"Well, *someone* did," Cynthia retorted heatedly, "and I assure you it wasn't me. The delivery note had our name and address, so naturally I thought it was for us."

"There must be two tons of the stuff here. Why the hell did you let them dump it in the drive? We can't get to either the house or the garage without going over the grass."

"What would you expect them to do with it, for heaven's sake? Look, it's no use ranting and raving, James, it's not *my* fault. Ring them up and complain if you want to, the phone number's on the delivery note."

"If you signed for it, they're not going to come along and meekly shovel it up again, are they? Anyway, they won't want to know on Saturday afternoon. In the meantime I can't get the car into the garage and the whole garden stinks like a farmyard."

"Dad!" The Jessels' sixteen-year-old son put his head round the front door. "There's someone on the phone asking to see the Merc."

Jessel turned. "What do you mean, asking to see it?"

"He seems to think it's for sale."

"Good God, I've only had it five minutes!"

"That's what I told him, but he says it's advertised in the *News.*"

"He must have the wrong number."

Jessel returned to glaring at the manure, but a moment later his son came out carrying the paper. "Look, Dad, he's right. It *is* in. 'Bargain price for a quick sale; phone Shillingham 59786.' "

Jessel snatched the paper out of his hand. "Has everyone gone mad today?"

Cynthia looked over his shoulder. "That's what it says, all right."

"I suppose you'll now tell me I must have put it in myself."

"No," she said slowly. "It looks to me as though someone is out to harass you. A follow-on to that letter."

Through the open front door came the ringing of the phone, and Lance resignedly went to answer it. "Probably someone else about the car," he said over his shoulder. "The phone'll be going all weekend."

Crombie's report on the London case proved inconclusive. Raymond had been found lying beside his car in a London back street, and despite exhaustive investigations, the only clue to come to light was the enigmatic note. It did not bode well for their own case.

Webb sighed and walked over to the wall-map. Rankin Road lay between two main thoroughfares, the High Street and the Marlton road.

"Surely *someone* must have seen something," he said disgustedly, "yet we've drawn a complete blank so far. No one noticed a strange car, either parked or driving into the Close. No one even heard the break-in. Granted, it was fairly late, but surely not *all* the local residents were in bed or dozing in front of the telly."

Crombie tipped back his chair, considering. "Let's try motive, means and opportunity. Means, we have a pretty good idea of, so how about opportunity?"

"Taylor says he left the pub alone, and at the moment there's no reason to disbelieve him. Incidentally, we did get a snippet from the barman; there's a woman who sometimes hangs around the darts players, and once or twice he's seen her leave with Baxter. She wasn't there on Wednesday, though."

"Suppose he'd given her the push? 'Hell hath no fury,' etc."

"It's possible. Anyway, since it seems Baxter was killed

immediately he got home, either his killer was waiting for him, or saw him arrive by chance and followed him into the drive on spec. But since he wasn't robbed, I don't really buy that."

"He could have picked up someone on the way home. Someone who, as soon as he got out of the car, turned on him. Baxter might have run round the back of the house, hoping to slam and bolt the side-gate on his attacker, but not had time."

"But again, was it a casual hitch-hiker or an acquaintance? That is, had he arranged to pick someone up?"

"If he had, he'd probably have mentioned it to his pals. You know—'Must be getting along, I promised old Geoff I'd pick him up on the corner at eleven-fifteen.' That kind of thing."

"It's worth asking them, certainly. As to motive, we've established it wasn't robbery, but can we really give credence to the April Rainers' 'crimes against humanity'? It's a bit hard to swallow."

"But it has to tie in with the London case. Unpopular victim, the April Rainers, and, as far as we can establish, identical MO."

"I agree, but we've run it through the computer again, and nothing else has emerged. From what you say, Snow Hill went all out that case, and came up with zilch. I thought we might have had a break there, but it's muddied the issue still further. And even if it *was* the April Rainers, who are they? Baxter might have known them personally without realizing."

"On the other hand, it *could* have been straightforward burglary. Suppose he simply heard a noise and went to investigate?"

"But whereas an interrupted burglar might well have coshed someone who surprised him—even, in these charming times, have stuck a knife in his ribs—a stocking just doesn't ring true. He'd want something he could use quickly and then scarper."

"OK. Someone was lying in wait for Baxter, with the stocking at the ready. Who?"

"I wish I knew. The Sandersons have a motive, but they were safely tucked up at their whist party twenty miles away."

"Had Mrs. Baxter any gentlemen friends? Anyone who might have set out to avenge her death?"

"If she had, we should be on to them soon. Partridge and Manning are working on it. In the meantime, all we can do is continue with routine inquiries."

"Cheer up, Dave, it's early days yet," Crombie said, returning the front legs of his chair to the floor. "Something's sure to turn up."

"You took a risk," Cynthia said, "phoning during the evening."

"Not really. If anyone else answered, I'd have said it was a wrong number."

"That's wearing a bit thin, you know. But I meant your wife. Won't she hear you?"

"Ah, that's the point. Anna's taken the kids to see her mother and they're staying overnight. I got out of it by pleading pressure of work. The old bat can't stand me, anyway." She heard the smile come into his voice. "I wonder if she'd be gratified to know her worst suspicions are correct? Anyway, here I am, and there you are, both on our own on a Saturday night. Any bright ideas?"

Cynthia felt her pulses quicken. Her affair with Robert was still a novelty, and the hint of danger added an irresistible fillip. But caution made her hesitate. "I'm not sure what time they'll be back."

"Then you come here. We'll have the house to ourselves."

"Yes, that would be safer. Oh damn—I've just remembered—I can't. There's a load of manure in the drive and I can't get my car out."

"Well, that's a new line on moats and drawbridges. The question is, can I get in?"

"It would be too risky to drive in, anyway. You'd better park up the road, under the trees."

"Fair enough. See you in half an hour, then."

She replaced the phone and paused to study her reflection in the mirror. The wide-eyed face looked curiously young, framed by prematurely grey hair in a straight, smooth bob. Appraisingly she turned from side to side, studying her image. Flat stomach, muscular arms and legs. Neck a bit crêpey, though—she must watch that. But generally, not at all bad—a conclusion confirmed by men's eyes every time she went out. So what was James's problem? Though glad enough of her decorativeness at official functions, his manner at home was one of controlled impatience—and she'd damn well had enough. No wonder, at forty-five, she'd fallen for Robert Kent's smooth talk.

They'd met at the tennis club. Robert's job as an estate agent meant he had no difficulty absenting himself from the office, and during the summer they'd formed the habit of driving out into the country for a drink. Before long, the drink had become only the preliminary to their activities.

Cynthia gathered that, unlike herself, Robert was used to conducting an affair, needing the excitement it added to his life. She didn't imagine she was in love with him, nor think for a moment that he loved her. But James had forfeited the right to her loyalty, and she needed the assurance that she was still attractive. And when, as it must, the affair fizzled out, it was comforting to know that no broken hearts would ensue. For the moment, though, and for their differing reasons, they suited each other, and Cynthia at least was content to look no further ahead.

Glancing at her watch, she went to prepare for his arrival.

5

THAT EVENING, over dinner with his girlfriend, Mark was steeling himself to cancel their date for the next day. In the event, it was she who raised the subject.

"Oh, I meant to tell you: Sally phoned and asked if we'd like to go sailing tomorrow. The forecast's good, so I said yes."

"I'm sorry, Jackie, you'll have to count me out."

She looked at him in surprise. They'd sailed on the reservoir several times, and he'd always enjoyed it. "I thought you'd want to go, but we don't have to if you'd rather not."

"No, I mean I can't make tomorrow at all. Something rather exciting's happened; I had lunch with the Harwoods today, and Felicity asked me to write her biography."

She frowned. "But you're not a writer. Not that kind, anyway."

"I know, but she says it's because I know her music so well. And with all due modesty, I do."

"But surely it's a full-time job, doing a biography?"

"That's the trouble. She wants me to take a year off."

Jackie stared at him. "Just like that?"

"It'd be a wonderful opportunity. I'd go with her on tour, be part of all the preparations and rehearsals, perhaps even be there while she's composing. Also, it would bring me to people's notice, which mightn't be a bad thing. She's a very sought-after subject, you know; professional biographers are queuing up for the chance to write it."

"Then why doesn't she let them?"

"I've no idea. Look, I haven't said I'll do it; it's not as simple as that. But the more I think about it, the more tempting it seems."

"But what about your job? They'd have to get a replacement, and you mightn't be able to slot back in again when it suits you."

"I know; it'd take a lot of planning. Anyway, to help me decide, I'm going to make a provisional start now, and take it from there. Which is why I can't see you tomorrow; I'm going round in the morning with my tape-recorder."

Jackie put her fork down. "Well, I think that's a bit much, expecting you to give up your weekends. You hardly get any free time."

"She's only here for a week or two, so we have to take what chances we can."

"Even when it means breaking a date? And what'll I tell Sally? It'll make me look such a fool."

"I'm sorry," he said again, an edge creeping into his voice. How often did he have to apologize?

Perhaps she heard it, too. She looked at him with her head on one side. "How old is this woman? Ought I to be jealous?"

He smiled. "Knocking fifty—not much of a threat."

But Camilla might be, he thought uneasily, aware that his attitude to Jackie had changed in the last few days. Her hesitant air, which he'd originally found attractive, now made him impatient rather than protective, and mannerisms he'd thought endearing had started to grate. She was possessive, too; her question on grounds for jealousy had been only part joke.

Damn it, he was being unfair. He had met Camilla only twice, and no doubt she had someone in her life already—maybe someone serious. It was foolish to let her dominate his thoughts to the detriment of poor Jackie, who had suited him well enough up to now. He looked up to find her watching him.

"I really am sorry," he said more sincerely. "Let's go to the cinema one evening instead."

"All right. But seriously, Mark, don't let this composer woman rush you into anything. You don't want to regret it later. What's she like as a person?"

He considered before answering, weighing up his own impressions with what Camilla had told him. "I'd say she's pretty tough: she's had to be; but you can't expect geniuses to be like ordinary mortals. See what you think yourself—you'll be meeting her on Wednesday."

As she would Camilla. Would warning bells ring, and if so, would they be justified?

Pushing all hypotheses from his head, Mark straightened and smiled.

"Now, let's change the subject. Would you like a dessert? The trolley looks tempting."

The phone by the bed started to ring, and Robert and Cynthia sprang guiltily apart. "It'll be about the car," she said breathlessly. "There was an ad in the *News*—a hoax of some kind."

"Aren't you going to answer it?"

"No point. It's been ringing all day." She smiled, tracing his mouth with one finger. "Ignore it—it'll stop soon."

"What did you mean," he asked idly, "about the wrong-number ploy wearing thin?"

"Well, you can't *keep* saying that, can you?"

"I haven't said it at all, yet."

"Yes you have. Twice in the last couple of days."

He frowned. "What are you talking about?"

The phone stopped ringing as abruptly as it had started. "Thank God," Cynthia said, shaking back her hair.

"Cynthia?"

"Well, you rang, didn't you, when James was here? And

we agreed from the beginning you'd only phone during the day."

"But apart from today, I've kept to that. I've never rung in the evening before."

She stared at him. "It wasn't you?"

"No, I've just said so."

"Then who was it?"

"A genuine wrong number?"

She frowned. "Twice? The first time was after Felicity Harwood's reception. The Conways had asked us back for drinks, and it was nearly twelve when we got home. The phone rang just as we were locking up. James answered it, and for several seconds, apparently, there was silence. Then a voice muttered something about a wrong number. When it happened again last night, again about midnight—we were in bed that time—he was really angry and talked of reporting it. But I persuaded him not to, because I thought it was you."

"Give me credit for some sense! Why the hell would I ring you at midnight?"

"I don't know." She paused, considering it from a new angle. "Perhaps it was part of this harassment campaign."

"*What* harassment campaign? You're talking in riddles."

"There was the ad about the car, and, as you saw, a load of manure's been delivered, which James swears he never ordered. He's had some anonymous letters, too."

"So someone's got it in for him? Well, well. What's he been up to?"

Cynthia lay down, pulling the sheet over her shoulders. Though she disapproved of James's business methods, she'd no intention of discussing them with Robert. "Goodness knows," she said.

"I read about him sacking the Broadshire *Life* editor."

"There was a personality clash."

"Pretty brutal, though, when she'd got the magazine back on an even keel."

Though she agreed with him, there was something distaste-

ful about his lying in James's bed criticizing him. A sense of
loyalty, illogical in the circumstances, nevertheless asserted
itself, and she turned devil's advocate. "There's no room for
sentiment in business," she said and, before he could reply,
added quickly, "What time is it?"

"Just after ten."

"You'd better be going. The boys may be back soon."

Downstairs, a door banged, and she shot upright, holding
the sheet against her.

"Cynthia?" a voice called. "Where the hell are you? Not
in bed already?"

"My God, it's James!" She turned frantically to Robert.
"Quick, into the bathroom, and take your clothes with you."

He scrambled from the bed, caught up his things, and had
only just reached sanctuary when the bedroom door burst
open and James stood there.

"Good Lord, you *are* in bed! Why didn't you answer the
phone? I tried to ring a few minutes ago. It's the opening
night of the new country club, and Douglas and I thought
you girls might like to go along."

He paused, taking in Cynthia's stillness and the sheet flung
back on the far side of the bed.

"My God, you bitch!" he said softly. "You've had someone here, haven't you? And in my goddamn bed, too. Where
is the bastard?"

Cynthia said, "James—no! No, you're wrong. I was just
feeling tired. Give me five minutes and I'll—"

But he strode to the bathroom door and started rattling the
handle. "Come out of there! At once, before I break the door
down!"

There was a pause and Cynthia waited, mouth full of heart-
beats. Then the door opened and Robert stood there. With
no time to dress, he'd wrapped a bathtowel round him, beneath which his bare legs looked knobbly and faintly ridiculous.

"And who might you be?" James demanded.

"I—I just—"

"Never mind." Robert flinched at the contempt in his voice. "Get the hell out of my house. Now. I'll have the details later."

"Can I—get dressed?"

"No, you damn well can't. Put your pants on and get out."

Robert retreated briefly and reappeared, clutching the rest of his clothes. With a helpless glance at Cynthia, he went quickly from the room.

James turned to his wife. "And you," he said deliberately, "can get your clothes on. You're coming to the club, whether you like it or not. I'm not going to be made a fool of in front of my friends. We'll discuss this later."

The next morning, Mark arrived at Fauconberg House as arranged and was shown directly to the music room, where Felicity awaited him.

"All set?" she inquired, as he set down his tape-recorder.

"I think so. I hope I don't make a hash of this; I've never done anything like it before."

"Nor I, but it's only a trial run, remember. We'll both be feeling our way."

"Right. Here goes, then." He cleared his throat and switched on the machine. "Were you born in this house?"

"No; we moved from across town when I was three, but it's the only home I remember."

Gradually, they settled into the interview, and to his relief Mark found that one question more or less naturally followed another. As he'd imagined, she could not remember a time without music.

"My mother sat me beside her at the piano when I was very small so I could watch her play. And when she finished, I was allowed to make my own attempts. By the time I was four or five I was making up tunes in my head, and not long afterwards picking them out on the keyboard."

"So parental encouragement was the spur for both you and Sir Julian?"

But she was quick to qualify that, and Mark learned to his surprise that their father had been actively discouraging.

"He was tone-deaf and hadn't the slightest interest in music, so he resented our 'wasting our time,' as he put it."

"But your mother persisted?"

"As far as she could. She came from a musical family, and though, with hindsight, her playing was only average, her father had been a conductor with the Shillingham Phil. Which is why Julian's appointment meant so much to her."

"But your father's attitude actually held you back?" Mark persisted.

"Oh yes. He wouldn't allow us to have private lessons, despite Mother's pleading. He maintained no one made a decent living at music, so it was a waste of time and money. It was only when we started school, Julian at St. Benedict's and I at Ashbourne, that we'd any professional tuition. It was like coming alive, for both of us."

"And you made up for lost time?"

"Yes, we sailed through all the exams and were soon taking part in school concerts, performing as soloists."

"You on the violin?"

"In the early days we both played the piano, but when I was about ten, my music mistress suggested I try the violin, and that was another rebirth. After that, I seldom had one out of my hand. I remember I used to play by the hour to gramophone records."

"And your father was won round eventually?"

She shook her head vigorously. "By no means. If anything, he was harder on Julian, insisting he go into a nice, safe profession like banking. No red-blooded male went in for music."

"And you?"

"By that time, I knew I wanted to compose. I pleaded to be allowed to read music at Oxford, where you can submit

compositions for your degree, but of course he wouldn't consider it. 'Whoever heard of a woman composer?' he'd say.
And since I showed no interest in anything else, he decreed I
should go to secretarial college. I would then, I was told, be
able to earn my living until I married, after which, with a few
babies to look after, I'd have better things to do with my
time."

Mark shook his head wonderingly. "So what changed his
mind?"

"Nothing did," Felicity said quietly. "He died when I was
fifteen." She looked up suddenly. "Can you imagine how I
felt? I'd been fighting him over music most of my life, re-
senting his stubbornness, thinking—you know how children
do—'I wish he was *dead!*' Then, suddenly, he was. For a long
time, I thought I was responsible, that I'd somehow wished it
on him."

"And his death changed your life?"

She nodded soberly. "I read music at university, then went
on to the Paris Conservatoire."

"It's frightening to think that had your father lived, you
might have been a shorthand typist!"

"Never! I'd have run away and earned money to pay for
lessons—scrubbing floors, if necessary. But it would certainly
have taken longer."

"It's good to know Ashbourne played such a positive rôle
in your music. Do you remember who taught you?"

"Certainly I do. Miss Grundy. She's still alive, in her nine-
ties now, and living in sheltered accommodation. I try to
keep in touch, but now that she has arthritis in her hands, she
can't answer my letters. I must call in to see her while I'm
here."

She stood up and walked over to a cabinet. "Here are my
diaries for the years I was at school. You might find them
helpful. There are other papers scattered about the house—
manuscripts, diplomas, that kind of thing. Just ask Elizabeth if
you'd like to see them."

She paused, looking down at him. "But I mustn't rush things. You might decide not to go ahead."

"We'll see," Mark said diplomatically.

Felicity laughed. "Well, that's enough talking for the moment. Let's go and have a drink before lunch, and we can have another session this afternoon. It'll be the only chance we'll have this week, but if you leave me the machine as you suggested, we can cut a few corners. Then, when the concerts are over and you've had time to write up what you have, you might have more idea of how you feel about it."

"Mrs. Dora Simpson? Chief Inspector Webb, ma'am, and Sergeant Jackson. Shillingham CID."

The woman stared at them with frightened eyes. "It's about Ted, isn't it?"

"That's right. Mind if we come inside?"

She glanced across the road at the twitching net curtains. "Well, I can't help you, I'm afraid."

"Nevertheless, we'd like a word," Webb said implacably, and she reluctantly stepped aside. The hallway smelt of roasting meat—lamb, Jackson judged, and his stomach growled in sympathy. Millie had a nice piece of pork this weekend, and it wouldn't improve, being kept hot all hours till he got back.

They were shown into the front room, and two teenaged children who were lounging on the sofa watching television were summarily dismissed.

"Now, sir." Mrs. Simpson stood in front of Webb, her hands nervously twisting together. "How can I help you?"

Webb studied her for a moment in silence. In her youth, she must have possessed a shallow, fleeting prettiness. Perhaps she didn't realize it had gone. This Sunday morning, her eyelids were painted an iridescent blue, her lips glistening plum, and her overbleached hair was tied with a pink bow.

"Are you widowed, Mrs. Simpson?" he asked gently.

"Divorced. Six years ago."

"How did you meet Mr. Baxter?"

She bit her lip and her eyes filled with tears. "It was at the pub—the Magpie. I used to go in sometimes with the girls from work, and I'd see him there. A fine-looking man, he was. I noticed him straight away, and he noticed me, too. Always looking in my direction. The men he was with used to tease him about it. Then one time when the other girls were on holiday, I went on my own and we got talking."

"When would that have been?"

"August, I suppose."

"Before his wife died?"

She flushed. "Yes. But she was no company for a man like that. Only thought of her children." She hesitated, then went on quickly. "You'll have heard about the court case, I'm sure, but you can't know the full story. She drove him to it, Mr.— Webb, is it? He wasn't a bad man."

If you were lonely enough and desperate enough, you could make yourself believe anything, Webb reflected. "How did he react to her death?"

"How do you think? He was shattered, of course. And while he was still reeling from it, that sister-in-law of his came and took the children. And they were all he had left!" Her voice rose with indignation.

"Did you ever stay at his house?"

She flushed, shaking her head. "I couldn't, because of the · kids. Mine, I mean."

"But you have been there recently?" She nodded. "Did he mention receiving threatening letters?"

Her colour deepened angrily. "He didn't need to—I have eyes in my head. The bin was overflowing with them. How can people *do* that? As if he hadn't suffered enough!"

"Did you read any of them?" Webb asked quietly.

"One or two, so I'd know what he was going through. They turned my stomach, I can tell you. Hate-mail, they call it. Ted said anyone whose name's been in the paper gets them, specially if they'd done what he was accused of doing, and even more so if they seem to have got away with it."

"Were they all much the same?" Webb asked casually. If Baxter had shown her the April Rainers' note, he might have made some comment, indicated he knew who'd sent it. A forlorn hope, but—

"There was one that was different," Mrs. Simpson was saying, and despite himself, Webb leaned forward.

"Yes?"

"Well, most of them went on about what they'd like to do to him—filth, mostly. But this one was more cold and—and factual, like. It read as if they not only *wanted* to kill him, but meant to. Oh!"

She looked up, aghast, her hand going to her mouth. Apparently for the first time, she'd made the connection between the letter and subsequent events. "You think they *did?* Is that what you're getting at?"

"It's possible. Tell me what you remember about that note, and particularly what Mr. Baxter said about it."

"Well, it was neat and tidy, not scrawled or made up from newspapers, like the others. And it was written in green ink. I remember, because you don't often see that. It was signed, too, but not a proper name that you could put a face to."

Webb and Jackson waited, not helping her, and a moment later she said triumphantly, "The April Rainers! That's it. It's a nursery rhyme or something."

Webb nodded. "Did he make any comment?"

"Said he'd be getting one from Bo-peep next." She mopped at her eyes. "That was Ted all over, trying to see the funny side, even of that." Which was a decidedly new slant on Baxter's character and, Webb suspected, rose-tinted with sentiment.

"But he'd no idea who sent it?"

"None whatever."

"Was he worried by the specific threat?"

"No more than the others." She shivered. "It must have been horrible, knowing all those people were out there hating you, but not who they were."

"He didn't think of telling the police?"

She gave a harsh laugh. "You must be joking! As if—" She broke off, remembering just in time who her visitors were.

Webb said smoothly, "When was the last time you saw him?"

Tears welled again. "Wednesday last week. We met at the Magpie as usual, and after the darts I went back with him for a while. We never guessed it was for the last time."

"So you didn't go to the pub this week?"

"No. Tracey wasn't well and I didn't like to leave her." Her eyes widened. "My lord! If I'd gone back with him this Wednesday like I did last—" She stopped, her face frozen in horror.

Webb glanced at Jackson, who nodded and closed his notebook. There was nothing further to be learned here.

"Thank you for your time, Mrs. Simpson," Webb said, rising. "Sorry to interrupt your preparations for lunch."

The teenagers lounged against the kitchen door, watching with sullen suspicion as their mother showed the detectives out. The smell of roasting lamb followed them down the path.

"Yes, Ken, before you mention it, we'll break for lunch."

Jackson grinned, and his step noticeably quickened. "Right, guv. Shall we stick with the Brown Bear? They've a new line in steak and kidney, Bob Dawson was telling me." And, whistling cheerfully in anticipation, he bent to unlock the car.

6

MARK WAS WHISTLING as he drove off the main road onto the uneven surface of the Oakacre estate. In the glow of a solitary street lamp the landscape looked positively lunar, but within a month or two, if the builders were to be believed, all would be transformed. The estate was to be an experiment, a carefully balanced selection of flats and houses aimed at encouraging a mixed community of young singles, families and retired people. A parade of shops and a surgery would also be provided.

Mark's house was one of only six so far completed. He had opted for a house rather than a flat because of the private lessons he gave two evenings a week. Unlike the flats, it had a separate diner, which he needed as a music room.

He parked in the muddy, unmade drive and let himself into the house. The afternoon session had gone quite well, though he was still feeling his way with Felicity. Knowing her music so intimately, it had come as a shock to realize he didn't know its composer at all. Several times when he'd anticipated her answer to a question, she had replied completely differently, and he'd had to realign the next one. Professional biographers, he reflected ruefully, would know better. Furthermore, he suspected that she'd expect to vet every page he wrote. His first rosy dream of accompanying her on concert tours had already been tempered by the realization that it would not be plain sailing.

He'd been reflecting on this when Camilla'd walked with him to his car. "Are you going to do it?" she'd asked.

"I don't know. I'd like to, but there are so many difficulties."

"She's paying you a great compliment, you know. For years, people have been wanting to write about her, have her speak to their societies, open concert halls or whatever, but she's dodged them all. It would be ironic if, the first time she actually *wants* someone to do something, he declines."

"I'm not just making excuses," he'd protested. "There really are obstacles. For a start, it would be at least a year before I could arrange a sabbatical and sort things out for my pupils." Yet if he turned down the chance, he was unlikely to see Camilla again. It was that thought which had prompted him to invite her to dinner on Thursday, when the panic of the school concert would be over.

"So you can pump me about my aunt?" she'd challenged him.

He'd grinned. "Partly."

"As long as it's only partly, yes, I'd like to. What time?"

"I have pupils from five till seven. Say, eight o'clock?"

"Fine. But I'll see you before that, at the school concert."

When, Mark reflected now, he would be in Jackie's company. Which could be awkward.

"Robert? Can you talk?"

"Cynthia—thank God! I've been nearly frantic, wondering what was happening but not daring to phone you."

"Is your wife back?"

"No, but they're due any minute. What *happened?*"

"Nothing, really. I imagine he's weighing the pros and cons of getting back at us, and the embarrassment if it becomes public."

"Public? My God, it can't! What about my job? And Anna, come to that. What did he actually say, when I'd gone?"

"Very little. He insisted I go to the Club with him, and I

was studiously polite the whole time. I was dreading our being alone, but the only reference he made was to ask your name."

"You told him?"

"Of course I told him. He could have found out easily enough."

"But God, Cynthia, what if he comes round here? Anna mustn't hear about this."

Cynthia held down her irritation. Was this the suave lover with a string of mistresses behind him? She said nastily, "Hasn't this happened before?"

"No, it bloody hasn't. You don't seem to realize my whole career could be up the spout. The senior partner's a stuffy old bird—Victorian values and all that. What's more, he's a friend of Anna's father, which is how I got the job."

"It's no use shouting at me, Robert. You're quite as much to blame as I am."

"Can't you talk to him—promise it'll never happen again?"

"That's for sure, at any rate," she said grimly.

"Hell, there's the car now. I'll have to go. Phone me at the office tomorrow. And for God's sake don't let him come storming round here."

The phone clicked in her ear and Cynthia dropped it with a clatter. Never a thought about her own predicament, having to keep up appearances in front of the boys and explain away James's withdrawal to the spare bedroom.

She sighed. Well, if you played with fire, you were likely to be burnt and it was no use crying about it afterwards. All she could do now was try to keep calm, and hope neither James nor Robert would do anything to precipitate disaster.

"I'm sorry, Mr. Jessel," the girl repeated over the phone the next morning. "We check as far as we can, but we'd no reason to think the ad wasn't genuine."

"What name and address was given?"

"Hold on, I'll check the computer." He waited, drumming

his fingers irritably on the desk. "Requested to go in Saturday's *Weekend News*. Name of Mr. J. Jessel, The Hollies, Stonebridge, phone Shillingham 59786."

Jessel swore softly. "What about payment? Was there a cheque?"

"It hasn't been received yet."

"You print advertisements without being paid for them?" It was not a practice he'd employ himself.

"Advertisers have the option of pre-payment, or being invoiced afterwards, which is slightly more expensive."

"I hope you don't expect *me* to pay for this?"

"I'm sorry, sir." Her voice was non-committal.

Impatiently, Jessel dropped the phone. Over the weekend, without warning, the tables had turned and he'd become a victim, the one to whom unpleasant things happened. It was a new and unwelcome experience which, under the impact of first the hoaxes, then his wife's betrayal, left him frustratingly helpless.

At least he could look into the former, try to track down the perpetrator. The problem with Cynthia was much more complex. And again, unbidden, the picture of her came to mind, wide-eyed on the bed with the sheet held against her, and the unprepossessing figure of her lover in the doorway.

Quickly he reached for the phone and dialled the stables. In response to his brusque questioning, the voice at the other end became defensive. The order'd come over the phone—a cart-load to be delivered to The Hollies, Stonebridge, payment on delivery. But the lady didn't seem to know about it and had no money on her, so a bill was in the post. What kind of voice had it been? Well, he couldn't rightly say. A gentleman, like.

It was useless to argue. In any case, though it was an infernal nuisance, the manure would at least enrich the garden, once he got round to clearing it from the drive. He'd enlist the boys' help—bribe them with extra pocket-money.

Which left Cynthia.

James was surprised how hurt he'd felt, though admittedly some of it was pride. Damn it, she had everything she could want: a beautiful home, two bright, healthy boys—and it wasn't as if he kept her short of money. She'd a generous allowance, and he always stumped up if she needed any extra. On the emotional side, he was on less sure ground, but after twenty years, she couldn't expect him to dance attendance as he had on their honeymoon.

She was still a striking-looking woman, though, with her lithe body and that premature grey hair. The thought that another man fancied her wasn't wholly unwelcome. Robert Kent, she'd said. They probably met at the tennis club; she spent a lot of time there. Surely she wasn't *in love* with that weed? He dismissed the idea out of hand. No, she was bored, that was all. The classic, bored housewife. But damn it, if he could toe the line, so could she. Traditionally, it was the man who strayed, but it had never entered his head. He was too busy wheeling and dealing to have time for romantic dalliance.

So what action should he take? he asked himself for the hundredth time. What *did* husbands do, for God's sake, in a situation like this? For some minutes he stared unseeingly at his blotter. Probably best to forget the whole thing. Least said, soonest mended. She and Kent would be pretty worried for a while, and serve them bloody-well right. But if he made a fuss and it got out, people would laugh behind his back. A cuckold inspired ridicule rather than sympathy, which was unfair, but there you were.

Yes, that'd be best, he told himself, pulling his papers towards him. He'd let them sweat it out for a while and say nothing. In the meantime, he'd take her to the Ashbourne concert as arranged; no point in throwing good money down the drain, and it did no harm to be seen among the wealthy and elite of the town. Then, later, he'd drop the hint that she'd better watch her step in future. And it mightn't be a bad thing to take her about a bit more. Keep the knot more closely tied.

Relieved to have resolved the problem, he pushed it aside and turned thankfully to the work awaiting him.

The next two days were, as Mark had anticipated, hectic ones. Felicity was to rehearse with the school orchestra on both Tuesday and Wednesday, but since Mark taught at St. Anne's on Tuesdays, he had to leave Tim Ladbury in charge. As soon as his classes were over, he hurried round to Ashbourne.

Felicity had gone and the orchestra disbanded, but Tim was still in the hall, sorting out music sheets. "How did it go?" Mark demanded breathlessly.

"Not so bad. A bit ragged at first, but Miss Harwood took it in her stride, and as the kids overcame their nervousness, it came together quite well. Tomorrow's rehearsal should iron out the remaining wrinkles."

Which, to his inordinate relief, Mark found to be the case. By four o'clock on Wednesday, when the rehearsal ended, anxiety had given way to excitement. Orchestra and soloist now melded perfectly; all would be well.

Unwilling to leave the hall, he lingered for a while, watching the caretaker and staff begin assembling rows of chairs for the evening's performance. White RESERVED tickets were laid on seats along the first few rows. Seated here would be Gwen and Hannah with their invited guests—Sir Julian and Lady Harwood, Camilla and Miss Matthews, the school governors, and directors of local companies who had already given generously to the Music-Wing Appeal. His parents were also invited, Mark remembered, aware that he should have contacted them.

He glanced at his watch; he'd the final lesson of the day in five minutes. Making his way to the music wing, he hoped yet again that Jackie and Camilla wouldn't come face to face during the evening.

It was the interval, and Felicity had not yet made her appearance. The orchestra had played well in the first half, both the Dvořák and the Rossini overtures being well received by the audience. Camilla had arrived with the other guests, but as Mark and Jackie were seated further back, she hadn't as yet noticed him. It was now, as the audience mingled in the dining-hall for refreshments, that they might unavoidably meet. In the meantime, his parents were approaching and he perforce introduced them to Jackie.

Making automatic replies to his father's comments, Mark kept a wary eye open for Camilla's approach. His mother, meanwhile, was chatting animatedly to Jackie, no doubt sizing her up as a possible daughter-in-law. Jackie herself had been rather quiet this evening, possibly sensing his own tension, but now, responding to his mother's evident interest, she was relaxed and smiling.

Taking advantage of their preoccupation, Mark glanced surreptitiously about him and caught sight of Camilla at the far side of the room. Murmuring his excuses, he moved in her direction. Perhaps a quick word now would deflect her from seeking him out later. But Camilla was engaged herself, surrounded by a crowd of friends, and all Mark managed was a stilted word with Hattie Matthews, who stood, large and uncompromising, on the fringe of the Harwood group. Then a bell rang, and the crowds began to drift back to the hall. The great moment had arrived.

It was a good ten minutes into the sonata before Mark let himself relax. It was going well, he thought elatedly. Tim was conducting superbly, and Felicity's playing was as vibrant and tender as always, giving no hint of apprehension concerning her accompaniment. He sat back, able at last to enjoy the lovely strains of music, as well as the fact that, despite all odds and after months of hard work, his Great Idea had at last come to fruition. Felicity Harwood was here, in her old school, and he had arranged it. It was a moment of supreme satisfaction.

The storm of applause as the final movement faded into silence was an indication of the enthusiasm of the audience, and time and again, as she acknowledged the applause, Felicity turned to the orchestra, inviting them to share it with her. Then the bouquets were handed up, sheaf after sheaf of glorious flowers, until there were too many for her to hold and one of the violinists came forward to take some from her.

What happened next was something Mark would go over again and again in his mind, trying to make sense of it. The final bouquet had been passed up and Felicity took it, smiling. Then, as she bowed yet again, she glanced down—at what? the flowers? the stage?—and gave a little gasp which, amid the continuing applause, was seen rather than heard. Her smile froze into a stylized rictus, the colour drained from her cheeks, and as he watched in horror, she slid to the ground, the flowers she held falling around her like wreaths at a wake.

The audience, gasping in dismay, rose as one man, those at the back of the hall craning to see what had happened as the last ragged scatter of applause died into a stunned silence. Mark found himself racing forward just ahead of the St. John Ambulance attendant. They reached the steps to the stage at the same time as his father, Sir Julian and Miss Matthews.

John Templeton said firmly, "Stand aside, please, I'm a doctor." And, to his son, "Draw the curtains, for God's sake."

Mark paused for one horrified glance at Felicity, lying crumpled at his feet with closed eyes. Was she *dead?*, he thought with incredulous horror, remembering Miss Matthews's warnings. Had it all been too much for her? Then he hurried into the wings and a moment later the heavy curtains, which no one had expected to be used today, swung ponderously across, swathing the anxious group bending over Felicity.

"It's all right," Dr. Templeton said, "she's coming round."

He stood up, and between them he and the attendant carried the inert form off the stage.

"It was absolutely terrifying, David," Hannah said later, as they sat drinking coffee in her flat. "I thought she'd had a heart attack, but John Templeton said it was a straightforward faint."

"So what brought it on? Heat? Excitement?"

"I don't know. She says she suddenly felt dizzy, and that's all she remembers."

"But?" prompted Webb, sensing her hesitancy.

"Well, no doubt that's what happened, if she says so. But I could have sworn that something had frightened her. Just for a moment, before she collapsed, she'd a look of total shock, as though she'd seen someone or something she hadn't expected to see."

"But she'd been bowing to the audience for some time, you said."

"Yes, and it was when she looked *down* that it seemed to happen."

"No cryptic message on the floor boards?"

"Not a thing."

"And nothing hidden in the flowers?"

"No. I had a quick look, under the pretext of rescuing them."

"Did she say anything as she came round?"

"Only 'Hattie.' That's Miss Matthews, her friend and agent."

"Was she there?"

"Yes. She bent quickly down and said, 'It's all right, Flick, I'm here.'"

"I wonder . . ." Webb mused, staring into his coffee-cup.

"What do you wonder?"

"Whether Miss Harwood was simply asking for her friend, or whether it had been something to do with her that caused the shock."

"I don't see how. She was just sitting in the front row with the rest of us."

"So what about Saturday's concert? Is it still on?"

"It seems so. Miss Harwood's set on it—it's the world première of her new work, after all, and Radio Three are broadcasting it live. It would be an awful let-down if it were cancelled."

"All the same, if she's not well enough to give it—"

"She insists she will be, but it's not just the concert, it's all the rehearsing beforehand. She's got two full days of it before Saturday—at her own insistence, I might say. What's so awful is that I can't help feeling responsible; perhaps it was too much to expect her to do two concerts in one week. I know Miss Matthews thought so—I'm sure she blames us for this."

Webb put down his cup. "I shouldn't worry too much. These professionals are pretty tough—they have to be. All the same, it would be interesting to get to the bottom of it."

Hannah smiled. "Once a detective, always a detective. How's the case coming along?"

"Not too well, and we're coming up to a week now. For all the clues he left, the murderer could have appeared out of thin air, done the dirty deed, and disappeared again, leaving no one the wiser."

"Which is presumably what happened last time, in London."

"If that was the last time," Webb said gloomily. "Crombie seems to think we might have a serial killer on our hands and there've been other, unreported cases. He's got me worried now, and I'm considering releasing the April Rainers angle to the press. Trouble is, we'd be inundated with calls from people wanting to get in on the act."

"How would you know which were genuine?"

"Oh, we'd hold back the details—green ink, copperplate writing, the style of wording. We could weed them out, all right, but it's pretty time-consuming." He sighed and stood up. "Anyway, thanks for getting my groceries, love. The way things are going, it could become a standing order."

Felicity's collapse was uppermost in both their minds when Camilla went to Mark's for supper the next evening. However, no immediate reference was made to it as she looked with interest round the house.

"And this is the music room," he finished, opening the door. "It was shown on the plans as 'diner, study or den,' but as you can see, they didn't allow much space."

"Enough for your easy chair, anyway," Camilla said.

"Oh, that's for the mothers, not me."

"You're chaperoned?"

"You can smile, but living alone caused quite a few problems. It's all right with the younger pupils, whose mothers bring them anyway, but there was no way I could be alone in the house with the others, either girls or boys, in the present climate. And the parents were no help. 'But Mr. Templeton,' they said, 'we *know* you!' Which, if they read their newspapers, they'd realize is no safeguard at all. Anyway, it's for my own protection as much as theirs—you can imagine how rumours could start. But fortunately my 'woman-wot-does' came to the rescue. Instead of 'doing' me two mornings a week, she comes in the evenings, during the lessons, and honour is satisfied."

"Doesn't she mind?"

"Not in the least. Says she's glad to get away from the telly. So I soundproofed this room for our mutual benefit—to muffle both 'the caterwauling,' as she calls it, and the sound of the Hoover."

He led the way to the living-room. "Let's have a drink, then supper will be ready. How's your aunt?" he added, as he poured her gin and tonic.

"All right. She's been at the concert hall all day, rehearsing. Hattie nearly went berserk, but there was no stopping her."

"They seem very close," Mark remarked, handing Camilla the glass.

"Yes, but don't go getting ideas. There's nothing unhealthy about it."

"God, I never—"

"Well, people do wonder sometimes, but if you're going to write her biography, you'd better get it straight from the start. They're close friends, that's all, who've known each other most of their lives."

"How did they meet?" Mark asked curiously, remembering his surprise at the seeming misalliance.

"At your precious Ashbourne. Hattie was very bright, but she was fat and plain and spotty, and a prime target for bullying. Girls can be as bad as boys, as you doubtless know. But when Felicity arrived, she rounded on the bullies like a miniature tornado, and because she was pretty and talented—as well as being bossy, even then!—the other girls took notice. Hattie was taken firmly under her wing, and has been devoted to her ever since."

"So they've always been together?"

"More or less. They were both at Oxford, but then Felicity went to study abroad, and Hattie stayed home. It's amazing, really; she had a first-class Honours Degree, but she didn't go for the glittering prizes. She used the time Felicity was away to train in various skills which she felt would be useful— management, accounting, even learning to type. Then, when Felicity came back and was ready to start professionally, Hattie was waiting, and they formed this formidable partnership. Hattie does all the donkey work—the booking, the accounts, the travel arrangements, leaving Felicity free to concentrate on her music. It works very well."

"To get back to yesterday, what exactly happened, do you know?"

Camilla frowned. "No, she won't be drawn at all. I felt something specific had caused it, but she insists she simply felt giddy."

"It came on very suddenly."

"Yes, and was over equally quickly. Father insisted on the doctor coming, but apart from slightly high blood-pressure there was nothing wrong, and by bedtime you'd never have known she'd been ill at all."

"As though she'd had a severe shock, and once it was over, recovered completely?"

"Exactly. And in face of the doctor's report, and her own insistence that she's fine, we'd no option but to let her play."

"Well, thank God she *is* all right."

"Yes." Camilla smiled slightly. "Now, do you think we could change the subject? It's nice to have a famous relative, but I don't want to talk about her *all* the time!"

"Of course. Sorry—end of pumping! Supper's ready, anyway, so if you'll move over to the table, I'll bring it through."

For the rest of the evening, he told himself, taking the dish from the oven, he wouldn't even mention Felicity. In the event, there was no temptation. They talked about their careers, their favourite books and plays, their hopes for the future, and by the time Camilla left, both were aware of foundations being laid. He would have liked to kiss her, but was afraid of rushing things. She solved the problem by reaching up to kiss his cheek.

"Good night, Mark. It's been a lovely evening. Thank you."

"We must do it again," he said, aware of sounding wooden. Then she was in her car, threading her way over the morass of rubble and builders' planks that was Oakacre to the conventional smoothness of Fenton Road, and her tail-light disappeared round the corner.

7

"WE'VE RUN DOWN another friend of Mrs. Baxter's, guv," Don Partridge reported the next morning. "The woman in the chemist's where she worked happened to mention her."

"Well done. Name and address?"

"Joan Parsons, 12 Priory Gardens."

Webb felt an instinctive jolt; that was the road where he'd lived during the eleven years of his marriage. He'd not been back since, though Susan had paid a nostalgic visit during her brief and ill-starred return to Shillingham.

"Right, Don, thanks; I'll go along and see her. No, I won't, though," he added, in the act of rising. "She might open up more to another woman. Ask Inspector Petrie to come in, would you." And, he told himself as he waited for Nina, his decision had in no way been influenced by the woman's address. Nina had a way of dealing with people which, during their first case together, might well have saved her life.* And now that Alan was back and Webb no longer had to share his office with her, the initial friction between them had mellowed to a mutual respect.

"Good morning, sir. You wanted to see me?"

"Nina, I'd be grateful if you'd visit one Joan Parsons, 12 Priory Gardens. The woman Linda Baxter worked with says she was friendly with her. I'll leave it to you what questions

* *Six Proud Walkers*

to ask, but it would be useful to know if there was any other man in Mrs. Baxter's life."

"Right, sir, I'll see what I can find out."

As the door closed behind her, Webb breathed an almost imperceptible sigh of relief.

Joan Parsons was a small, bustling woman in her late forties. When Nina identified herself, she led her into the neat front room, with the clock in the exact centre of the mantelshelf and identical ornaments on either side.

"Sit down, Inspector. Can I get you a coffee? I've just made some."

"That would be welcome, thank you."

As Mrs. Parsons poured from the pretty flowered pot, she said steadily, "I don't have to ask why you're here."

"I suppose not," Nina said gently. "Had you known Mrs. Baxter long?"

"We met at ballroom dancing, when we were seventeen. There used to be classes every Saturday in the old Alexandra Hall. It was knocked down when they built the Arts Centre."

"I remember the Alex," Nina said. "I went to ballroom dancing, too."

"Did you really?" Mrs. Parsons's nostalgic expression brightened. "What a coincidence! Was it still Nettie Briggs when you were there?"

"Yes—good heavens! Nettie Briggs with her beehive hair-do! I'd forgotten all about her."

"Just fancy that! Well, that's where I met Linda, and we became friends from the word go. I was her bridesmaid when she married Ted."

Nina said carefully, "Did she confide in you, when the marriage went wrong?"

The woman's face clouded. "Not at first. And when she did, I had to promise not to tell Norma. That's her sister, over in Ashmartin. Linda didn't want her worrying. Mind, I didn't like promising. In my opinion, it would have been all

to the good if Jim had gone round to sort Ted out. It made
my blood boil, to see what he did to Linda. She wasn't the
same person at all. Such a happy, laughing girl, she'd been."

"Did she never consider divorcing him?" Nina had first-
hand experience of an unhappy marriage.

"She would have done, if it hadn't been for the kids. She
decided to hang on till they were old enough to understand.
Now, poor little blighters, they've neither a mum nor a dad."

"I can understand how she felt, though." Not as long-
suffering herself, Nina nonetheless felt guilt at having de-
prived her own daughter of her father. "It's a tremendous
decision to take," she added sombrely, "and if unhappiness
had sapped her confidence, it makes it even harder."

"That's it exactly—he'd destroyed her confidence. She had
a lovely voice as a girl, and used to sing solos at church
concerts and things. But Ted was jealous of anything that
didn't involve him, and he made her give it up. Later, when
the kids started school, she begged him to let her take up
singing again, but he wouldn't hear of it. 'I'm not having
latch-key kids,' he told her. The nerve! Linda was always a
devoted mum. And to crown everything, he told her her
voice had probably gone anyway. But that's the way he was,
always putting her down. Called her all sorts, till she almost
came to believe him. Yet she was still a capable, pretty
woman, even at the end. Well, I mean, Mr. Chadwick would
hardly—" She broke off, a red tide suffusing her face.

"Mr. Chadwick?" Nina repeated innocently.

"I shouldn't have said that. I'd be grateful if you'd forget
it."

"Mrs. Parsons, I know Linda Baxter was your friend, but
this is a murder inquiry. Please tell me about Mr. Chadwick."

"There's nothing to tell," the woman replied. "It never
came to anything."

"Who is he?" Nina persisted.

"The gentleman where she worked. At Chadwick's the
chemist's, in Westgate."

"He was interested in her?"

"He would have been, if she'd given him half the chance. He noticed some bruises on her face which she'd not managed to conceal. That was how it started. I mean, Mr. Chadwick's a gentleman, and he'd never have spoken if he thought Linda was happily married."

"Did she tell him she wasn't?"

"She didn't have to—he has eyes in his head. He lives with his mother above the shop, and one day when she was very shaky after a bad bout with Ted, he took her upstairs for a cup of tea. Ever so gentle, Linda said he was. But as I say, nothing *happened.*"

"Did she ever meet him outside working hours?"

"She couldn't, because of the children. As it was she only worked part-time so she could be home when they got back from school."

"But even so, Mr. Chadwick became fond of her?"

"Yes. I know she found it a comfort, even though she didn't give him any encouragement. And I'm the only one who knew about it. I shouldn't really have mentioned it."

"Have you met him yourself?"

"Not *met,* but I've seen him in the shop. I was naturally curious, after what Linda'd said. Seemed a very nice gentleman."

"Have you seen him since her death?"

Mrs. Parsons shook her head. "No, I—I couldn't bear to go near the shop."

"I'm sorry—of course not. So you won't know how he reacted?"

The woman said dully, "How d'you expect him to react, poor man? He just had to take it, like the rest of us."

Unless, Nina thought, he'd decided to avenge her. Still waters sometimes ran deep.

"Will you be going to see him?" Mrs. Parsons asked anxiously.

"The Chief Inspector will."

"He won't mention my name, will he? I shouldn't like Mr. Chadwick to think I'd been tattling."

"The Chief Inspector's very discreet," Nina said.

The chemist was a tall, thin man with receding dark hair and a prominent Adam's apple. Webb caught a flash of panic in his eyes as he introduced himself.

"If it's about Mrs. Baxter, your men have already been here," he said. "We told them all we know."

"Just a few more questions, sir," Webb said easily. "Is there somewhere we could talk?"

A customer had come in after them, and was being served by the woman assistant. With obvious reluctance, Mr. Chadwick led them to the dispensary behind the shop.

"Could you tell me, sir," Webb began, "if Mrs. Baxter confided in you about her husband's treatment of her?"

Chadwick's face suffused with colour, and the Adam's apple jerked hysterically. "I was Mrs. Baxter's employer, not her confidant," he said stiffly.

"But you were fairly close to each other, weren't you?"

The man's indrawn breath was loud in the quiet room. "I don't know what you mean," he said faintly.

"I understand, for instance, that on at least one occasion you took her upstairs for a cup of tea?"

Chadwick swallowed convulsively. "How—how—"

"Mr. Chadwick, I'm not suggesting anything improper took place, but in the circumstances some reference must have been made to the bruises she'd suffered. Surely you noticed them?"

The chemist passed his tongue over dry lips. "Yes," he said quietly, "I noticed. It grieved me to see her in such a condition, a gentle, charming woman like that."

"So I repeat, did she confide in you?"

"Not really, no. She—played it all down. I offered to go and speak to her husband, formally, of course, as her employer, but she became quite hysterical at the idea."

"Did you ever meet Mr. Baxter?"

"No. Just as well, as I'd have been hard put to be civil to him."

"So you never went to her home?"

"Never."

"Not even to run her back after work?"

He shook his head. "We really were on a work basis, Chief Inspector. Since you have apparently heard something, I admit I'd have liked our relationship to be deeper, but it was not to be."

Webb said casually, "Where were you on the evening of the fifth, sir?"

"The fifth?"

"A week last Wednesday."

"At home with Mother, I imagine. We spend most evenings together."

"And your mother can confirm that?"

Chadwick raised an eyebrow. "I imagine so, if it's necessary. Apart from—oh. A week last Wednesday, you said?"

"That's right, sir."

"Then I'm mistaken. The first Wednesday in the month, Mother plays duplicate, at the bridge club."

"And what do you do?" Webb asked quietly.

The man's nervousness had returned, but Webb couldn't be sure if the date held any significance for him. "Occasionally I go to the cinema, but I usually stay home and read or listen to the radio."

"And last week?"

"I believe I stayed in."

"So you were at home when your mother returned?"

"Oh, definitely. I always am. She likes to give me a detailed account of the evening's play over her cocoa."

"What time does she get back?"

"About quarter to eleven. They stop play at ten-thirty."

And at eleven o'clock, Ted Baxter was still at the Magpie.

So it hadn't been the chemist lurking in his garden. Another avenue of inquiry cut off, Webb thought wearily.

"Thank you for your time, Mr. Chadwick," he said, and Jackson followed him dispiritedly out of the shop.

"Where now, guv?" Jackson asked, as they paused on the pavement outside.

"Back to the nick, I think. We'll get this lot written up, then have a bite of lunch."

"You still reckon Baxter's death is tied up with his wife's?"

"I wish I knew, Ken. Heaven knows, we've not much to go on."

Each wrapped in his own thoughts, they turned off West-gate into Franklyn Road. Ahead of them was the Arts Centre, of which Shillingham was justly proud. Completed ten years ago, it was a vast complex which included art gallery, library, concert hall-cum-theatre, a high-class restaurant, and two enormous rooms which were leased for exhibitions. Today, there were large placards outside blazoned with the name of Felicity Harwood, who would be performing the world pre-mière of her new work the following evening. Webb, glanc-ing at them as he passed, hoped nothing would cause her to faint this time.

They had barely walked a hundred yards past the Centre when a sudden commotion broke out behind them, and they spun round in time to see a youth running towards them with a handbag under his arm.

"Not your lucky day, chummie," Webb said under his breath, as Jackson caught the boy without difficulty. He was breathing fast and wriggling like an eel but Jackson held him fast.

Webb looked back along the pavement. A small blond woman was hurrying towards him, relief on her face. "Oh, thank you!" she exclaimed as she came within speaking dis-tance. "I thought I'd seen the last of it."

"You're in luck, ma'am. He ran straight into the arms of the law."

The boy renewed his efforts to escape, but Jackson, for all his slightness more than his match, cautioned and arrested him. The woman's eyes widened. "You're police?"

"Chief Inspector Webb and Sergeant Jackson. The station's just round the corner; we won't keep you long."

"Oh, but there's no need for that, surely? I have my bag back, after all." She reached out to take it, but Webb held on to it.

"I'm afraid there's a procedure to be followed, ma'am."

For a moment, he thought she was going to argue. Already a knot of interested bystanders had gathered. Perhaps aware of them, the woman said crisply, "Very well, if I've no choice."

With the two men on either side of the thief, holding firmly to his arms, the small procession turned the corner into Carrington Street.

Having handed over their charge to be documented and searched, Webb turned to the woman. He'd intended to leave Jackson to deal with her, but something about her was needling his memory and on impulse he led her to an interview room himself.

"I'll need your name and address, ma'am, and an account of exactly what happened."

She sighed. "Very well. I'm Felicity Harwood, and I'm staying with my brother at Fauconberg House, Hampton Rise."

Webb put his pen down. "Miss Harwood—of course. I should have recognized you. It's a pleasure to meet you. I'm only sorry it's in such circumstances."

She smiled. "Thank you."

"I hope you've recovered from your—indisposition?"

"At the school, you mean?" She made a dismissive gesture. "It was only the heat. I felt a fool, causing such a fuss."

Regretfully stifling his curiosity, Webb returned to the matter in hand. "Now, Miss Harwood—the bag-snatch. What exactly happened?"

She shrugged. "I hardly know, it was all so fast. I'd been at the hall rehearsing for tomorrow, and was on my way home for lunch. As I came down the steps, this boy cannoned into me. I thought at first it was accidental, but then he made a grab for my bag and was off. And I'd only had time to give a shout when you caught him."

"Have you ever seen him before?"

She looked at him blankly. "The thief? Of course not."

"You're not, for instance, in possession of something he might want?"

"Money, you mean? There's about fifty pounds in there."

"If I may?" Without waiting for permission, Webb opened the lizard handbag and tipped its contents onto the desk. He heard her faint gasp, but she made no protest. As he'd supposed, there was nothing suspicious there, and he replaced the articles in the bag.

"I trust you're satisfied, Chief Inspector?" There was an edge to her voice. She reached again for her handbag and this time he let her take it.

"Perfectly, madam, but you'll appreciate we have to treat everyone the same, even illustrious ladies such as yourself. Now, once we have the man's details—"

She said quickly, "I told you—I don't want to take it any further."

"May I ask why not?"

"I've got my property back, after all."

Webb said heavily, "Not many people are so lucky. We're plagued with bag-snatchers and shoplifters at the moment, and if their victims refuse to press charges when they get the chance, we're not going to get anywhere."

"I'm sorry, I realize I'm not being public-spirited, but my only thought is to forget the whole business as soon as possible. Anything like this weighing on my mind would affect my playing, and I can't risk that. In any case, when it came to court, I should probably be abroad." When he didn't speak, she added more placatingly, "Look on it as giving a young offender another chance. Perhaps it will be a lesson for him."

Webb sighed. "If I can't change your mind, then I must ask you to sign a statement of withdrawal, and that'll be the end of the matter."

She duly did so, then looked up at him, her lips twitching. "You're disappointed in me, aren't you, Chief Inspector?"

"I'd have preferred you to press charges, yes."

"I'm sorry. I do appreciate your help, and I hope you understand my reasons."

"We have different priorities, I suppose. Good luck with the concert, Miss Harwood. At least you'll have nothing to distract you now."

When Mark returned home that evening, he poured himself a drink and settled down to look through Felicity's diaries. It was a task he'd been intending to perform all week, but what with the school concert, the evening lessons, and Camilla's visit yesterday, there had been no opportunity. Now, however, it was Friday, and though Felicity would be unable to see him tomorrow, with the second concert in the evening, she would expect him on Sunday for another interview, and he should be as up-to-date as possible in his research.

The earliest diary, its leather scuffed and pages bent, was inscribed on its first page: "Felicity Harwood, aged ten and a half, Fauconberg House, Hampton Rise, Shillingham, Broadshire, Great Britain, the World, the Universe." The writing was in pencil, and difficult to decipher. Mark flicked through it quickly, finding nothing of interest in accounts of homework and hockey matches. The name "Hattie" appeared at regular intervals.

He smiled ruefully, acknowledging a naive hope of indications of burgeoning genius on every page. How old was she before music became the centre of her life? It was well before her father's death, which occurred when she was fifteen, she'd said. He selected what he guessed to be the relevant diary and began to go through it. The writing was neater and better formed, in ink now, and there were references to musical scores studied, lessons with Miss Grundy, one or two sulky comments about parental restraint. Then, on 14 April, instead of the usual closely written entries, only two lines appeared. "Spent the day with Hattie. When I got home, Mummy told me Daddy was dead."

It had happened during the Easter holidays, and family mourning appeared to have clamped down. Over the next week, only a couple of lines appeared for each day, one of which mentioned the funeral. Mark had reached the beginning of the summer term when the doorbell clarioned into his concentration.

Camilla? he thought on an irrational upsurge of hope. He hurried to the door, to find Jackie on the step.

"Oh—come in," he said, trying to sound welcoming.

"Not interrupting anything, am I?"

"I was reading through Felicity's diaries." Thank God she hadn't come yesterday; that would have taken some explaining. And hard on the relief came the uncomfortable awareness that Jackie deserved an explanation of his changed attitude.

"How is she?" she was asking, as she settled on the sofa in her usual corner. "I presume tomorrow's concert is still on?"

"Yes, it seems it was just a dizzy spell, with no after-effects."

"Thank goodness for that. But since you dashed off to minister to her, we didn't arrange what time you'd pick me up."

Mark, pouring the drinks, hesitated. If he said nothing, he'd again be in the position of trying to keep the girls apart —which, after last evening, would be even more difficult.

"Are your parents coming?" Jackie continued, seemingly unaware of his silence. "I thought they were sweet—we got on really well."

Mark said gently, "Jackie, there's something I have to say." He handed her the glass, unwillingly meeting her wide, inquiring eyes. "I—think it would be better if we didn't see quite as much of each other for a while."

"Why?" she asked flatly.

"Because I'm no longer sure how I feel."

There was a silence. He seated himself on the edge of his chair, staring into his own glass. He was burning his boats without any real idea of Camilla's feelings, but even if they were negative, his own precluded a continuing association with Jackie.

"Is there someone else?" she asked in a small voice. He nodded, not meeting her eyes. "But she's too old!" she burst out. "You said so yourself!"

For a moment he stared at her in bewilderment. Then he said, "It's not Felicity, Jackie."

"Then who? You've not had time to meet anyone else."

"It's her niece. Look," he went on quickly, before she could speak, "I'm not saying there's anything between us, because there isn't really. But—"

"—you'd like there to be," Jackie finished bleakly.

"I'm sorry, love. It just—came up out of the blue."

"Does she feel the same?"

"I've no idea."

"Suppose she doesn't?"

"Even so," Mark said awkwardly.

"I see. So that's it?"

"Well—in a way. We can still—"

"Don't," Jackie said rockily, "for God's sake, don't say we can still be friends."

"No. Sorry. But at least let's go to the concert as we planned." He felt he owed her that much.

She shook her head quickly. "I suppose she was at the last one, the girl? What would you have done if we'd met?"

He shrugged. "Jackie, I feel badly about this."

"Not as badly as I do. And just after meeting your parents, too. I really thought—" She drank hastily from her glass.

"I'm sorry," he said helplessly. She stumbled to her feet and set down the empty glass.

"Well, no point in hanging round here. Goodbye, Mark. It's been fun."

He guessed her control was running out, and followed her silently to the front door. "Goodbye, Jackie. Thanks for everything. And I really am sorry."

She gave a little, choked sound, and disappeared into the darkness. Mark closed the front door. *"Hell!"* he said vehemently. Why couldn't people fall in and out of love at the same time? Morosely he went back to the living-room and the discarded diaries.

It was later than he intended when James Jessel left the golf club that evening. Not, God knew, that there was much to hurry home for. Cynthia was still being wary. He'd give her another week or so, then move back to their bedroom. The guest-room bed, though fine for overnight visitors, was not as comfortable as his own. As to her gigolo, James hoped he was having a thoroughly worrying time, wondering what action would be taken.

He got into his car, aware that he shouldn't have had that last glass of whisky. One of the penalties of living at Stonebridge was the proximity of County Police Headquarters just down the road. Better take it gently.

It had started to rain, and headlights coming in the opposite direction glinted blindingly on the wet windscreen. James swore to himself. He'd have to leave the car out again, too, since he still hadn't got round to shifting that manure. It would be even more unpleasant after the rain. Bloody hell— that, and the phone calls still coming in about the car, and those damn-fool letters. Cynthia was right, someone must have it in for him. Well, it was irritating, but he wasn't going to lose any sleep over it.

Here was the old stone bridge that gave the district its name. Easy now, and make sure nothing's coming the other way. He tooted as he drove onto it. Some hundred yards farther on, Police Headquarters stood foursquare, its windows a blaze of lights in the wet darkness. As he passed it, he sketched a mock salute. And here, thank God, was his own turning.

He took it rather faster than he'd intended, and immediately jammed on the brakes, feeling the wheels spin on the soft ground. Bloody hell, what was going on? Almost opposite his gateway a car was parked, facing up the lane. The bonnet was up, and in the glare of his own headlamps, he could see a figure peering inside.

James was no Good Samaritan, least of all in rain and darkness. On the other hand, unless the car was shifted, he couldn't get into his own drive. Turning up his collar, he reluctantly got out of the car and walked round the other one to the open bonnet.

"What seems to be the trouble?" he asked. They were the last words he spoke. As he bent in his turn to look into the car's maw, something hit him on the back of the head. He was already losing consciousness when the lethal stocking went round his neck.

8

ONCE AGAIN, it was a milkman who discovered the body, though fortunately not the same one. By the time Webb and Jackson arrived, a plastic tent had been rigged over it—more to protect the investigators than the deceased, since rain had fallen relentlessly throughout the night.

"Same MO, Dave," Dick Hodges said over his shoulder. "Asphyxiation, and the ligature removed. Additional bump on the back of the head, though that might have occurred earlier."

"Who is he?"

"Owner of the house up there." Hodges jerked his head in the direction of the wrought-iron gates. "James Jessel. Been in the news recently, hasn't he?"

Webb grunted. "This his car?"

"Right. Driver's door on the latch, headlights and ignition switched on."

"So he was almost home when something caught his attention, and he got out to have a look."

"Just like the last one," Hodges confirmed.

"Who's up at the house?"

"The wife, and two lads in their teens. The milkman went there for assistance, so I didn't see their initial reactions."

"OK, Dick, we'll go and have a word."

"What's the betting he got a letter, too?" Jackson said cheerily, as they set off on foot towards the house. After some eighty feet the drive forked, the right-hand branch leading to a garage a few yards away. Immediately in front of the fork, and therefore blocking access to both house and garage, was a considerable quantity of malodorous manure. The only way past it was by walking on the soaking wet grass, which drenched their shoes. "A nice way of saying 'Welcome!'" Jackson grumbled.

In front of the house, the drive widened to a large gravel sweep into which two old-fashioned street lamps had been set, one on either side. The house itself was handsome, though too ornate for Webb's taste. The front door was resplendent with columns, a white iron balcony ran along the front at first-floor level, and a profusion of hanging baskets filled the porch. Ducking to avoid them, he rang the bell.

The woman who opened it was striking-looking, her soft, pale grey hair framing a youthful face with large, deep-blue eyes that now regarded him fearfully.

"Mrs. Jessel?" She nodded. "Chief Inspector Webb and Sergeant Jackson."

"Please come in." Her voice was low and husky, but that might have been due to the circumstances. The hall floor was highly polished, and scattered with oriental rugs. Against the wall opposite, an elegant Regency table held a bowl of rust and copper chrysanthemums, whose reflection in the mirror behind them doubled their glowing splendour.

The woman led the way to the drawing-room. It was furnished in pale grey and lemon, with a high marble fireplace, its grate screened by another huge vase of flowers. Gracious living, no doubt, Jackson thought, but it could hardly be described as homey.

"Mrs. Jessel," Webb began, "I'm extremely sorry about your husband. I appreciate you're still in shock, but unfortunately we can't hold back on our questioning."

"I understand," she said quietly. "Please sit down." She seated herself in a brocade armchair, hands folded in her lap like a child.

"How did you learn of your husband's death?"

"From Sam—the milkman. He rang the bell and hammered on the door till I woke up."

"What time would that have been?"

She shrugged. "A quarter to seven?"

It was now eight-thirty. "When did you last see your husband?"

"After dinner last night. He went to the club as usual."

"What club is that?"

"Larksworth Golf Club. But it's social as well—they have a billiards table, and a bar, of course."

"Did he seem in good spirits?" Watching her closely, Webb saw her hesitate.

"Much the same as usual."

"Weren't you concerned when he didn't return home?"

She flushed hotly. "He was often late back. I never waited up."

Queer sort of marriage, thought Jackson.

"You must have been alarmed, though, when you woke to all that knocking and found he still wasn't with you."

Her flush deepened. "Actually, Chief Inspector, my husband had been using the spare room for the last few days. He'd a lot of business worries and wasn't sleeping well. He didn't want to disturb me."

Was that the true explanation? Webb wondered. If so, why the heightened colour? He changed tack. "Had your husband any enemies, would you say?"

"Oh yes." There was bitterness in her voice. "Any number. You can't be as successful as he is without making enemies, or so he tells me." She paused. "Told."

"Had he received threats of any kind?"

"Yes, though he didn't take any notice."

"In what form?"

"Anonymous letters mostly."

Webb sat forward. "Did he keep them?"

"No, but he left one crumpled on the breakfast table, and I read it." She shivered. "It was signed 'The April Rainers.'"

Webb let out his breath in a long sigh. "When did he receive it?"

"Last Friday." She looked up suddenly, staring at him as her face paled. "My God," she whispered, "it came true!"

"Mrs. Jessel, this could be vital. What did the letter say? Can you remember?"

"Yes, it was going round my head all day. The misquotation intrigued me, because I didn't know if it was deliberate. It said, 'You are found guilty of evil deeds which assault and hurt the soul. The death sentence will be carried out in eight days.' I worked out that would be Friday. And it *was!*" She stared at him, horror-stricken.

"What did you mean by misquotation?" Webb asked gently.

"Part of it comes from the Prayer Book, but it should be evil *thoughts,* not deeds."

"And you thought that significant?"

"Yes. Evil thoughts would assault your own soul, evil deeds someone else's."

Webb digested that for a moment. Then he said, "Your husband never thought of going to the police?"

"No, I told you. He said successful people always attract cranks, and the only thing to do with anonymous letters is ignore them."

"You say he'd received others?"

"There'd been a couple earlier in the week, but I don't know what they said. In fact, there's been quite a harassment campaign going on—phone calls, hoax advertisements in the paper, that kind of thing."

"And your husband had no idea who was behind it?"

"I don't think so."

"Had you?" The suddenness of the question startled her, which might have been why she coloured. She shook her head in silence.

"Did he have any dealings with Mr. Ted Baxter?"

She frowned, trying to think where she'd heard the name.

"Oh, the man who was murdered. Not that I know of. Why?"

Webb hesitated, but it would be public knowledge as soon as the press got it. "Because he also received a note from the April Rainers."

She looked at him blankly. "You mean they're a kind of— hit squad?"

"All we know at the moment is that your husband seems to be the third person they've threatened who's died on the day appointed. The first was in London a couple of years ago."

"And you've no idea who they are?"

"Not as yet, I'm afraid." He paused. "I suppose it's no use asking if you heard anything last night?"

She shook her head. "As you saw, it's quite a long drive."

"Where does that lane lead to?"

"Only up to the farm, but it's not wide enough for tractors, so they don't use it much. They've another entrance along the main road."

"So you're virtually the only people who use the lane?"

"Yes."

Then anyone lying in wait for Jessel would run little risk of waylaying the wrong person. But what, in heaven's name, was the connection between Jessel the tycoon and Baxter the wife-beater, let alone Thomas Raymond in London?

"Mrs. Jessel, did anyone have a particular grudge against your husband?"

"As I said, he was always upsetting people. The most re cent thing was the Broadshire *Life* takeover. He didn't keep to the agreement and made people redundant. Obviously, there was a lot of resentment."

Jackson made an appropriate note in his pocketbook.

"Forgive me, but I have to ask this: was your marriage happy?"

She met his eyes defiantly. "I didn't murder him, if that's what you're wondering." Then the fight went out of her.

"I'm sorry," she said quietly. "I know you're only doing your job."

"So?"

"What's happy?" she asked enigmatically. "James was one of those men whose work is more important than his family. I knew that when I married him, so I've no cause for complaint."

"But you felt—neglected?"

"I suppose so."

"Did you build up interests of your own?"

"I enjoy sport. I play squash and tennis all the year round."

"But not golf?"

She smiled slightly. "No, we didn't fraternize."

"You're not aware of your husband having any women friends?"

She shook her head. "No, that's one thing I am sure of. You can rule out the possibility of jealous husbands."

She sounded very positive about it. Did it mean Jessel had little interest in sex, even with his wife? Was that, perhaps, the reason for the retreat to the spare room? And if so, had she looked elsewhere?

Cynthia said in a low voice, "To a lot of people, Chief Inspector, my husband seemed inconsiderate, impatient, intent on pursuing his own interests without caring whom he hurt. But basically he was a decent man, extremely generous and, when he exerted himself, good company. I think that in his own way he was still fond of me. As I was of him."

Sudden tears overwhelmed her, and she reached helplessly for a tissue. It was true, she thought wretchedly, and she'd have given anything to be allowed to live the last week over again. If only James hadn't found her with Robert! With hindsight, she knew there'd been hurt behind his rage, bewilderment at her betrayal.

Aware that the policemen had risen to their feet, she tried to control herself. "I'm sorry," she murmured.

"No, Mrs. Jessel, it's we who are sorry, to intrude on your

grief. Unfortunately it's unavoidable. And now, perhaps we could have a word with your sons."

The elder boy, aged eighteen, was subdued and monosyllabic, with little to contribute. Though he was obviously shocked, he seemed the kind of boy who was wrapped in his own affairs and took little interest in the life of the family. Fortunately, however, the younger one, Lance, was either more observant or spent more time at home. He was quite willing to enlarge on what his mother had referred to as a 'harassment campaign'—the false advertisement in the *News*, the unwanted load of manure and a series of late-night phone calls.

"We thought someone had it in for Dad," he ended.

"Any idea who it could have been?"

The boy looked up suddenly, an expression of shock on his face, and Webb guessed that for the first time, he was making a connection between the hoaxes and the murder.

"Well?" he prompted, but Lance shook his head violently and would not be drawn. Webb studied the downcast face. He knew something—something which perhaps loyalty to his father—or mother?—prevented him from disclosing.

He said quietly, "You want us to find the killer, don't you?"

Lance nodded without raising his eyes.

"Then if you know anything—anything at all, even if you don't think it's relevant—you must tell us. It could be vitally important."

The boy looked up at last, anguish in his eyes. For a long moment Webb held his gaze, willing him to give in. Then, with a whispered "I'm sorry," Lance looked away.

Webb stood up, motioning to Jackson. "All right, Lance. But think about it. And if you change your mind, you can either phone or call to see me at Carrington Street. I hope to hear from you soon."

Mrs. Jessel was hovering in the hall when they reached it. It was apparent she'd been weeping again. Webb said gently,

"Is there anything we can get you before we go? Anyone you'd like us to contact?"

"No, thank you. I'll be all right." She opened the door for them, and with a last look at the silent boy behind her, the policemen left them to their grief.

It was still raining. When Webb and Jackson reached the gate, Hodges had some news for them.

"Come and look at this, Dave," he said, leading him to the far side of the lane. The ground sloped up fairly steeply, covered with a tangle of gorse and low-growing bushes. Protected by them from the worst of the rain, a set of tyre prints was scoured deep into the mud.

"I'd assumed at first that he took the corner wide and went up on the bank. But when we got round to studying them, it's clear the marks weren't made by this car—the tread's entirely different. What's more, it looks as though another vehicle was parked just in front of Jessel's—see that patch of oil? At some stage it drove up the lane to the farm gateway— those aren't Jessel's prints either—reversed into it, and came back down, going up on the bank here on the way out."

"And the only reason to do that," Webb said slowly, "would be to get round Jessel's car, which was blocking the lane."

"Exactly. Another thing—see those thorns? A couple of them had minute traces of blue paint on them. They'd only have made a faint scratch—the owner probably hasn't even noticed it—but they should tell us the make and age of the car."

"Well done, Dick. Let me have the results as soon as you can. Oh, and by way of confirmation, Jessel received a note from the April Rainers."

Hodges nodded. "That figures. But they're stepping things up, aren't they? Two in ten days, for Pete's sake!"

"And both on our patch," Webb said gloomily. "Why couldn't they have stayed in London?"

"Perhaps they cover the country. Contract killers—'Stocking for Hire.' "

Mrs. Jessel had suggested something similar. "Well, the time has come to release it to the press. We need to know if, God forbid, there have been other cases." A sudden breeze shook down a spray of water from the trees overhead. Webb grimaced and turned up his collar. "In the meantime, we'll leave you to it. Come on, Ken, we'll make a start with the Broadshire *Life* people."

Felicity Harwood stood at the window, staring out at the sodden garden. The lawn and flower-beds which, last week-end, had still held an echo of summer, were now dank and bedraggled under a cloak of fallen leaves. Autumn was unmistakably here.

She sighed. That card tucked into the bouquet had really thrown her. Stupid to let it get to her like that; she must put it out of her mind, forget it.

Behind her on the bed, the muffled sobbing continued. Holding down her irritation, she turned back into the room.

"Come on now, Hattie, that's enough. Wash your face and you'll feel better." She stood looking down at the heaving shoulders, the straight, tousled hair. Weeping did nothing for Hattie's already plain looks. "It'll be all right, you know," she added with a touch of impatience. "It always is."

Hattie eased herself up on the bed like a beached whale, gulping in a valiant attempt to stay her sobs. She reached for a handkerchief and blew her nose.

"Sorry, Flick," she said in a clogged voice. "You're right, of course. It's only—"

"Yes, I know. I'm on edge, too, but we can't give in to it. Now, splash some cold water on your eyes and we'll go down for breakfast. And hurry—I've a final rehearsal at ten."

The other woman blundered to her feet, and Felicity gave

her shoulder a pat as she passed en route to the bathroom. "It'll be all right," she repeated reassuringly. "I promise." Hattie gave her a wan smile and did not reply.

"There were eight redundancies among senior staff," Jackson said, reading from a list. "And a lot more lower down the scale. The diarist, Terence Denbigh, collapsed and died soon afterwards. I remember reading about it."

Webb took the list from him and ran his eye down it. Gaby Fenshawe, ex-editor. He knew the name; Hannah took Broadshire *Life,* and any time he'd picked it up, he'd made a point of reading the editorial. Good stuff, and what's more, the girl had done a resuscitation job and saved the magazine from the brink of folding. It was poor reward to be handed her cards, and he bet it rankled. How deeply? Though whatever her resentment against Jessel, it was difficult to imagine a connection with Ted Baxter. Still, they had to make a start somewhere.

"We'll begin with Gaby Fenshawe," he said.

The Fenshawes lived in a small Victorian villa, which had been lovingly restored to make an attractive home full of character. Gaby opened the door to them, a diminutive figure in cords, an oversize sweater and bare feet. She apologized for the latter on learning their identity. "I thought it was the paperboy wanting to settle up," she explained. "Do you mind coming into the kitchen? I'm timing a pie, and if I leave it, I'll forget it. Anyway, it's more comfortable in there."

She settled them at a large scrubbed table and set two steaming mugs of coffee before them. An open fire burned in the grate and a delicious smell of baking filled the air. After the bleak wet outdoors, the warmth and cheerfulness of the room were doubly welcome.

Their hostess checked the oven, then turned to them with a smile. "Now," she said, "what can I do for you?"

Webb looked back at her assessingly. If she was bitter over

her dismissal, she gave no sign of it. Her smile was friendly, with a hint of humour, and lit up her small, olive-skinned face. She wasn't wearing make-up, and after her baking efforts, her nose had a slight shine. He said flatly, "You won't have heard about Mr. Jessel?"

She turned down her mouth in a comic gesture of gloom. "Oh, him! What's he been up to now?"

"He's got himself murdered."

There was complete silence. A look of incredulity came over her face—genuine, Webb could have sworn. "Oh no! When? What happened?"

He remained silent, and she went on, "But why come to me? I can't help you; I haven't seen him for weeks."

A man's voice in the hall saved Webb from replying. "Gaby? Was that someone at the door?"

A tall, dark man appeared in the doorway and surveyed them frowningly. He had a thin, clever face and he too was barefooted and in casual clothes—jeans and an open-neck shirt. It was Saturday morning, after all.

His wife said in a strained voice, "Nat, these gentlemen are from the police. James Jessel's been murdered."

Watching him closely, Webb could have sworn he caught a fleeting glimpse of panic in his eyes. Fenshawe swallowed nervously. "But that's terrible. When did it happen?"

"Sometime last night," Webb said. Then, casually, "Where were you both, last night?"

Gaby gasped and moved to her husband, presenting a united front. "Look, what is this?" she demanded, as he stood silent beside her. "What right have you to burst in and start questioning us as though we were criminals?"

"We hardly 'burst in,' Mrs. Fenshawe," Webb said mildly. "Nor are we treating you as criminals. You don't have to answer, of course, but it's a pretty simple question."

Fenshawe said quietly, "There's no secret about it. We went to the cinema." There was a nerve jumping in his cheek, and Webb continued to regard him, though he addressed his wife.

"You must have been resentful about losing your post in the takeover."

"I was hopping mad, but that doesn't mean I'd stick a knife in him. Anyway, I've got another job now; I heard yesterday. Does that dispose of my motive?"

Fenshawe, aware of the continuing steady gaze, shifted his weight uneasily.

Webb said, "There was a lead-up to the killing. Phone calls, poison-pen letters, unsolicited goods." He leaned back in his chair and sipped the cooling coffee, his eyes not leaving the man's face. Sweat had broken out on his hairline, and his teeth, fastening convulsively on his lip, drew a bead of blood. His all too obvious nervousness contrasted strangely with his wife's indignant innocence.

"Well," she said stoutly, "it was nothing to do with us. I'm sorry he's dead—no one deserves to be murdered—but I'm not going to weep crocodile tears for him. He made a lot of enemies for himself."

"Mr. Fenshawe?"

"I—only met him once. I can't say I cared for him. In fact, I thought him an arrogant bastard, if you want the truth."

"Oh, we certainly want the truth, Mr. Fenshawe. By the way, what colour is your car?"

Fenshawe stared at him. "My car? Blue. Why?"

"May we have a quick look at it?"

But when, at Webb's request, it was driven out of the garage, no scratch was visible to the naked eye. No matter; if the paint sample corresponded to last year's Ford Escort, the tyres would be the deciding factor.

"Well, thank you for the coffee," Webb said. "And if either of you remembers anything you'd like to tell us, you know where we are."

"Why did you let him off the hook, guv?" Jackson demanded, as they drove away. "He obviously knew something, and he'd have cracked in another minute or two."

"I decided to leave it to his wife," Webb replied. "She was as conscious of his nervousness as we were, and was surprised by it. She'll get it out of him, and provided he's not the killer, she'll tell us about it."

"But he *could* be the killer. An evening at the cinema's no alibi for a late-night murder, and he has the right colour car."

"Don't worry, Ken. I'll have a tail put on him just in case, but I'm willing to bet either he or his wife will show up at Carrington Street within the next twenty-four hours. Let's see if I'm right."

9

ONCE AGAIN, it was the interval before Felicity's performance, and this time, Mark was alone in the crowded foyer.
Gwen, hearing the tickets were at a premium, had decided
not to attend. "I'll have heard her play once," she'd explained diffidently. "It's only fair to let someone else have a
chance. It's different for you, dear, being such a devoted fan
and so much more musical than I am. And you'll have Jackie
for company."

In which, of course, she was mistaken. At least he'd handed
back her ticket, Mark thought, and wondered guiltily where
she was this evening. No more worrying, anyway, about
keeping the two girls apart. He'd seen Camilla in the box
with her mother and Miss Matthews. Sir Julian, of course,
was conducting, and although the first half of the concert had
been well received, the audience was clearly here for the
world première. BBC microphones were in position, and everyone had the excited air of being present on a historic occasion.

"Hi there," said a soft voice, and Mark turned to see Camilla.

"Hello. Can I get you a drink?"

"I've had one, thanks. I was looking for you. Aren't you
with anyone?"

"No, my—er—friend couldn't come."

"We thought you looked rather lost, in the middle of a row

with no one to talk to. Mother wondered if you'd like to join us in the box? There's plenty of room."

"That's very kind of her—I'd love to."

"Let's get back then, out of this crush."

Lady Harwood greeted him graciously, and there was a nod and brief word from Hattie Matthews. The latter was pale and austere in a severely styled black dress, which emphasized the poor condition of her skin.

"You'll have to excuse Hattie," Camilla told him. "She suffers agonies at Felicity's concerts, but refuses to stay home and listen on the radio."

Mark looked at the woman with a raised eyebrow. "Are you afraid she'll make a mistake?"

"Nothing so rational," Hattie replied. "But since I suffer enough stagefright for both of us, she's free to concentrate on her music."

Mark glanced down at the glossy programme. "I see there's a new photograph for the occasion."

"Is there?" Camilla turned the pages of her own programme. "I hadn't noticed."

"Quite right, Mr. Templeton. We have them taken every three years or so; Felicity has a horror of people finding her older than her photograph."

A rustling in the auditorium indicated that the audience was returning and the second half of the concert was about to start. Mark settled back with a feeling of anticipation as the orchestra filed in. The great moment was at hand.

Nor was he disappointed. By the end of the first movement, it was clear that in this latest work, the composer had surpassed herself. Melody, composition and interpretation had reached a new level, and Mark knew, with a sense of awe, that he was hearing truly great music, worthy to stand alongside accepted masterpieces. All the more incredible, then, that the same slight figure centre-stage, whose superlative playing lifted the music to a dimension all its own, should also have had the genius to conceive it.

As the final movement came to a close, the auditorium was hushed. Then, with a swelling roar of approbation, everyone rose, many people with tears streaming unashamedly down their faces as they clapped in a frenzy of homage. In the years to come, Mark thought, applauding wildly himself, they would tell their grandchildren they'd been present at this performance. Four, five, six times, Felicity returned from the wings to bow and smile. Then came the bouquets, and Mark sensed a prickle of apprehension in the box beside him. If she should faint again—

But no incident marred tonight's acclamation. Reviewers were now leaving the auditorium to phone in their superlatives, and up in the gods the younger element had started stamping their feet, the rhythmic rumble underlying the continuing applause.

Mark turned to Camilla. "I'll have to go, too, and make my report," he said. "Tell Felicity—" He broke off with a smile, and shook his head. "Never mind. Perhaps by tomorrow I'll be able to find the words."

She nodded and squeezed his hand. "See you then."

Excusing himself to Lady Harwood, he left the box.

When Webb arrived at Hannah's flat, the broadcast of the concert had just finished. He settled himself in a chair as she switched off the radio. "That was quite fantastic," she said. "I taped it for you, since you missed the school performance."

"Thanks; I'll look forward to listening to it. Actually, I met Miss Harwood yesterday. She had her bag snatched, would you believe."

"Good heavens—how awful!"

"Not so awful. The thief ran straight into Jackson's arms. It was all over in a matter of minutes."

"What did you think of her?" Hannah asked curiously.

"A lady with a mind of her own. I couldn't persuade her to press charges—it would seemingly interfere with her music.

Despite her slight frame, I'd say there's a core of steel running through her."

"Gwen was telling me she wants Mark Templeton to write her biography."

"Who's Mark Templeton?"

"Gwen's nephew. I must have mentioned him—he's one of our music masters."

"Well, it would be quite a feather in his cap."

"Except that he's had no experience of that kind of thing. Gwen doesn't know quite what to make of it. It would mean his taking leave of absence, and so on. Quite an upheaval."

"Is he going to do it?"

"He hasn't decided. But you're right about her strong will. She seems determined he should, and has offered him a dummy run while she's here. Every spare minute, he goes round to the house with his tape-recorder. Still, enough of that. How are things with you?"

"Pretty lousy. We've had another April Rainers-linked murder."

"Oh, David, no! Who was it?"

"I'm surprised you haven't heard. James Jessel, of Jessel Enterprises. He—"

"Mr. *Jessel?* But he was one of our guests at the school concert!"

"His wife says he'd a lot of enemies. There'd been other letters as well, but since they were destroyed they can't be checked against those Baxter received. The April Rainers' might not have been the only duplication."

"How was he killed?" Hannah asked shakily.

"Same as the last one. A ligature round his neck. Ten to one it'll turn out to have been a nylon stocking."

"I just can't take this in. I was chatting to him for several minutes, thanking him for his donation to the fund." She drew a steadying breath. "Have you any leads on the first case?"

"Nope. Damn it, if people would only report poison-pen

letters, we might have a chance. We'd certainly have been on
the alert this time, given Jessel protection, and possibly been
able to prevent his death. But it's no use thinking of that
now. We're releasing their name to the press, so let's hope
that will curtail their activities."

The Sunday papers certainly gave full rein to the story. WHO
ARE THE APRIL RAINERS? ran one headline, and, beneath it,
a two-column spread: "Two men have been murdered in the
last week in Shillingham, Broadshire, after receiving death
threats signed by 'The April Rainers.' A similar case was reported in London two years ago. Now the police, who stress
that all anonymous letters should be reported, are anxious to
discover whether other unsolved murders may have been
preceded by such death threats. The first victim . . ."

Mark, about to leave for Fauconberg House, dropped the
paper on the hall table. He'd read it properly this evening.
Unpleasant, though, to think of some gang prowling round
Shillingham. He hoped Camilla wasn't out alone after dark.

Felicity was waiting for him in the music room. She looked
older than usual, with purple shadows under her eyes and
fine lines between nose and mouth.

"How are you?" he asked, and it wasn't mere formality.

"Exhausted, but I daren't admit it. Hattie always said I
shouldn't do two concerts in a week. I gather you enjoyed
last night?"

"It was out of this world."

"I've been reading the reviews. As usual, yours is one of
the most perceptive." Her mouth twisted. "It was the only
one, I noted, to refer to me as 'one of the leading composers
and violinists of the century.' "

Mark looked surprised. "But surely I read something very
similar in—"

She held up her hand. "A word's difference, Mark—and a
world of difference. The others called me a leading *woman*

composer. Do they refer to Britten as a *man?* An artist shouldn't require that qualification; it's so belittling.''

"I'm sure it's not meant to be."

"I'm not saying it is—it just comes naturally to them. But not, thank God, to you. Is it any wonder I want you to do the book?''

She bent and retrieved a folded newspaper from the stack on the floor. "I particularly liked what you said about weaving together the serenity of Romanticism with the challenge of the present day. You see, that was precisely my intention.''

She leant towards him, letting the paper slide back to the floor. "Shall I tell you where I first had the idea for the piece? It was in Glastonbury, on a summer afternoon two years ago, when I saw a plane flying over the Tor. Nothing unusual, but it struck me as being symbolic of our fast-moving computer age co-existing with our most ancient and mysterious past. And you somehow picked that up. It must have been telepathy.''

Mark said awkwardly, "It was also an inspired performance. I doubt if anyone else will dare play it for a while.''

"Yes, it was good. We'd had a disastrous rehearsal in the morning, though. I'm notoriously difficult to work with; even Julian says so. But I *know* the way it should sound, and I won't accept any other interpretation. However, enough of last night; let's get back to business. Here's the cassette you left with me last time—I've filled it, so you can give me another if you've a spare.''

They worked together for the rest of the morning, Mark asking questions, Felicity filling out her answers to encompass subjects on the fringe of the query. Several times, as she recounted past happenings, Mark found himself surprised by a streak of ruthlessness, and once, sensing his reaction, she said caustically, "I've never pretended to be sweetness and light, Mark. I've had to fight to get where I am—as you know, it's man's world—and I've made some enemies in my time.''

"Enemies?" he repeated, with raised brow.

"Yes indeed. When you're well known and successful, it's inevitable, but I don't let it worry me." Had she known it, she was paraphrasing James Jessel.

During the lunch break, Mark had no chance for a private word with Camilla, but following the afternoon session, he again walked with her in the garden. The ground was saturated from the previous day's rain, the dahlias flattened into the soil, their proud heads twisted beneath them. "How's it coming along?" Camilla asked idly.

"Slowly; we're still discussing her childhood. It's surprising how difficult her father was about her music; if he hadn't died fairly young, she might never have got going. It doesn't bear thinking about." He bent, trying without success to prop up a drooping dahlia. "What was it? Heart attack?"

"Oh no. In fact, he didn't actually *die,* he was killed in a rail accident. I think the fact that it was an accident made it harder to accept. Felicity told me once she was afraid she might have *willed* him to have one, because he wouldn't let her study music."

"Yes, she said as much to me."

"Do you think you'll do the book?" Camilla asked.

"I honestly don't know. I'm waiting till she goes back to London and I've a chance to go over what I've got. Then I'll weigh it up and see how I feel. To be honest, it'll be a relief when this trial period's over; trying to combine it with teaching is quite a strain. Did you know she invited me to go to Edinburgh with her? Unfortunately, though, there's no way I can fit it in. What happens, when you're given the Freedom of a City?"

"I'm not sure, but it's a tremendous honour; she's only the third person Edinburgh's awarded it to in twenty years. They invited her to appear at the festival, too, and even though she couldn't make it, an entire evening was devoted to her music."

Their walk had brought them full circle to the house, and

they went inside for Mark to say his goodbyes. As he was leaving, Hattie appeared at the top of the stairs.

"Oh, Mr. Templeton—I'm glad I caught you. I've just found an old school photograph you might like to see."

She came hurrying down the stairs and, a couple of steps from the bottom, stumbled suddenly as her ankle gave way. Mark and Camilla started forward, but they were not in time to catch her. With a sharp cry, she fell down the remaining steps, landing heavily with her ankle bent beneath her. The noise brought the other three hurrying from the drawing-room, and it took a concerted effort to raise her. By the whiteness of her face and the unnatural angle of her foot, it was clear some quite serious damage had been done.

"We'd better get you to Casualty," Sir Julian said. "They'll need to take X-rays."

Hattie said between gasps, "They can do what they like as long as I'm mobile for Tuesday. I don't intend to miss Edinburgh."

"Can I help at all?" Mark asked, holding the photograph that had been the cause of the trouble.

"No, we can manage, thanks."

He would only be in the way if he stayed; there were enough of them to do what was necessary. "I'll phone later and see how she is," he said.

The news when he rang that evening was much as he'd expected. Several bones in the foot had been broken, and Hattie would be immobile for some weeks. Edinburgh, naturally, was out of the question.

"That's what's upsetting her most," Camilla told him, "but there's nothing anyone can do about it."

"I feel at least partly responsible," Mark said, "since she was hurrying to show me the photograph. Do please give her my sympathy."

So that was that, he reflected, replacing the phone. "The best-laid schemes . . ." He'd send round some flowers in the morning.

At Carrington Street, the phone calls had started to come in. Now the job would be to sort out the genuine ones from the cranks.

"The devil of it is," Webb told the impromptu gathering in his office, "they'll all have to be looked into. Still, we'll give the most likely ones priority. Any ideas on those?"

Nina said, "As you instructed, every caller was asked to describe the notes in detail. So far, only three seem genuine, mentioning the style of message, green ink and so on. One call came from Cardiff, one from Liverpool and one from Leeds."

"These 'Rainers' certainly get about," Webb commented. "Well, we'll start with those three. Don, you and John to Cardiff, please; Bob and Steve to Liverpool; and Harry and Fred to Leeds. Let's hope you all have more luck than Inspector Crombie here. We'll see what we get from these before moving on to the less likely ones."

"I suppose the rest will be the usual attention-seekers," Dawson said dismissively.

"Not necessarily. If someone close to you is murdered and the killer isn't caught, it's almost impossible to come to terms with it. Some of these poor devils are probably clutching at straws, telling themselves such a note *might* have been received, and hoping to renew police interest in their own cases."

Webb's phone rang and he reached forward wearily to answer it. But at the sound of the voice he straightened, and threw Jackson a triumphant glance. "Yes, of course, Mrs. Fenshawe. I shall be here for the next hour or so, if you'd like to come over."

Gaby Fenshawe was more subdued than when they'd last seen her, and more formally dressed. She was accompanied by her husband, who fiddled continuously with his tie.

"Chief Inspector," she began, when they were all seated,

"you said yesterday that you thought the—the harassment campaign against James Jessel was connected with his death."

Webb had not said precisely that, but he waited in silence.

Her colour deepened. "We felt we had to come and tell you that it wasn't."

Webb raised an eyebrow. "Perhaps you'd explain how you know that?"

Fenshawe straightened in his chair. "Because I was responsible for it," he said abruptly. "And I very definitely didn't kill him."

"So what *did* you do, Mr. Fenshawe?"

"Made one or two late-night phone calls—the heavy breathing kind—advertised his car for sale, and had some manure delivered."

"And wrote letters?"

Fenshawe flushed in his turn. "Yes. That's why we decided to come. But I didn't sign them 'The April Rainers.' I didn't sign them at all."

"What did the letters say?"

"That he was an arrogant, selfish bastard who didn't care how he treated people. It was true, and although I'm not proud of what I did, I don't take back a word of it."

Those earlier letters Mrs. Jessel had mentioned.

"It was how he treated my wife that really got me," Fenshawe burst out, when Webb remained silent. "And old Terry Denbigh, too. Jessel literally caused his death—the shock was too much for him. Gaby wouldn't take him to a tribunal, but I didn't see why he should get off scot-free."

Webb transferred his gaze to her. "Did you know anything about this?"

"No," she answered in a low voice. "Nothing."

"Very well, Mr. Fenshawe. Since harassment is a civil, not a criminal, offence, it'll be up to Mrs. Jessel to decide whether she wants to take you to court."

Fenshawe's high colour paled. In his haste to clear himself as a murder suspect, such a possibility hadn't occurred to him.

"In the meantime," Webb continued inexorably, "if you'll accompany the sergeant to an interview room, we'll get things sorted out."

"I'm going to be interrogated?" Fenshawe looked wildly from Webb to Jackson and back again. "But why? I've told you everything now, I swear it!"

"That's as may be, but you withheld evidence last time you were interviewed, so we want to make sure nothing else has slipped your mind."

There was another interesting phone call that day, from DI Francis in London. "I've managed to trace that gang I was telling you about, sir. They *are* in your neck of the woods, camping on Chedbury Common. That anywhere near you?"

"Right on our doorstep. Thanks, Inspector, we'll go straight over and have a word."

Webb looked across at Crombie. "Let's hope this is the break we've been waiting for."

Chedbury Common lay on the far side of the village from Shillingham, stretching for several miles on either side of the road. Together with the woods that bordered it to the west, it was a favourite haunt of both courting couples and dog-walkers. They saw the caravans as soon as they came out of the village.

"The County Council'll be after them," Jackson remarked with satisfaction. "They're always having to move gyppos from this site."

He pulled off the main road, and the two men walked across the short, scrubby grass towards the camp. A small, surly group stood watching them approach. To Webb's jaundiced eye, they looked like gypsies themselves. The men were bearded and dressed in ubiquitous jeans and sweaters. The women had long hair and long skirts, which blew around their ankles in the strong breeze. Two of them were holding babies, and a few children played some yards off, throwing a stick for a yapping black dog.

One man, apparently the spokesman, stepped forward. "Yes?" he said. "Can I help you?"

Surprisingly, his voice was cultured, the assured accent of the stockbroker belt.

"We'd be glad of a word, sir, if you could spare us a minute," Webb said, instinctively broadening his own accent in the hope of being taken for a country copper. Which, come to think of it, he was.

"As long as you're not going to move us on," the man said with a grim smile, and the subtle condescension in the tone told Webb his bait had been taken.

"Are you planning to stay long, sir?"

"Until our work here is finished."

"And what work would that be?"

"Much the same as yours, Constable. Righting wrongs and preventing wickedness. You might almost say we're partners." He paused. "I presume you *are* the police."

"We are, yes, sir," Webb agreed, meekly, even gladly, accepting his demotion. He was careful not to glance at Jackson.

"Then come inside and ask your questions," said the man benevolently, and, as the group parted to let them through, he led them up the steps into the nearest caravan. It was clean and pleasantly furnished, night-time bunks having been converted into comfortable sofas. There was a table, chairs, even a bookcase, and a small cooker and sink were tucked away at one end. All mod cons, Jackson thought admiringly. He might hire something like this for their next holiday.

He and Webb took the seats indicated to them, while their host remained standing. A psychological advantage over the bumpkins, Webb thought.

"You might have heard," he began, "that we've been having a spot of bother this last week. Two murders, in fact, within a few miles of each other."

The man shook his head sadly. "It's an evil world, Constable, despite all our efforts. But from what I read in the papers, we needn't waste time mourning the victims."

"Their families might not agree with you, sir."

"True. Innocent people frequently suffer from the wrongdoing of others. What we need—and off-the-record you probably agree with me—is the reinstatement of capital punishment. An eye for an eye, as the Good Book says. When you come down to it, that's the only real deterrent."

Would a murderer advocate a return to the death penalty? Webb wondered with interest. "How do you set about your own work?" he asked, adroitly dodging the issue.

"We approach wrongdoers and try to make them see the light. Occasionally, if they refuse to listen to us, we have to punish them."

"In what way?"

Caught up in his own oratory, the man had forgotten to whom he was speaking. But bumpkin or not, this policeman wouldn't condone taking the law into one's own hands.

"Nothing that need worry you," he said dismissively.

"You write to them, like? Urge them to—to repent?" Webb hoped he wasn't overdoing it. Beside him, Ken make an odd sound which he turned into a cough.

"That kind of thing, yes, but we also visit them when we can. A face-to-face discussion is much more productive."

"Could I ask, sir, if you visited either Mr. Ted Baxter or Mr. James Jessel?"

"No, I'm afraid I can't help you there."

He'd hardly have admitted it, anyway. But there was no sign of a blue car among those parked on the common.

"As it happens," Webb continued, "Mr. Baxter was in Chedbury the night of his death. You might even have seen him in the Magpie."

"We don't hold with strong drink, Constable," the man said reprovingly. "It's over twenty years since I entered a public house."

Which didn't rule out his following Baxter home, though in fact the Magpie was at the other end of the village.

"Those letters you write—do you sign them?"

"Of course."

"*What* do you sign them?"

"Ah, I begin to understand—we've read the Sunday papers. You're wondering if we're the April Rainers? Strangely enough, it's not the first time we've been asked that, and I give you the same answer I gave your colleagues. No, we're not, but we applaud what they're doing. This world needs cleaning up in every sense—morals, personal habits, surroundings." His eyes began to sparkle with fervour as he launched into his spiel. "There's dirt and litter everywhere, indicative of the moral decline of society dating from the permissive sixties. We must shake things up, make it a fit place for our children to grow up in."

All of which was most enlightening, but time was getting on.

"I'm sure you're right, sir. Now, perhaps you'd be good enough to give me your name, and your address, too, if you have one."

The man frowned. "I can't see why that's necessary."

"Just routine, sir," Webb said soothingly.

"If you insist. I'm John Fletcher and when I'm not travelling I live in Surrey." He gave an impressive address which Jackson took down.

"How long have you been camped here?"

"About ten days, though I can't be certain. Time means little to us when we're on a mission."

"And how long will you be staying?"

The man shrugged, answering with a question. "Another ten?"

Not if I can help it, Webb thought. "And none of your—friends—know anything about the April Rainers?"

"Not a thing," said Fletcher confidently.

It would be pointless to interview them at this stage—

they'd all talk in the same clichés as their leader. But a spot of hard questioning at Carrington Street would not go amiss.

"Well, sir," Webb said, getting to his feet, "we won't detain you any longer. Thank you for your cooperation."

"A pleasure, Constable. Always glad to help the law."

Except when it moves you on, Jackson thought. The group outside had dispersed, and the two men walked in silence back to the car. Only as they closed the doors did Jackson say with a grin, "Ever thought of going on the stage, guv?"

"I hoped he might let something slip, Ken, but he was too sharp. All we got is that they go round haranguing people, and without a formal complaint—unlikely in the circumstances—we can't touch them for it."

"You think they're in the clear regarding the murders?"

"We'll have them in, but I'm very much afraid so."

10

ON THE MONDAY MORNING, Webb received a phone call from Cynthia Jessel. Her voice was determinedly light, attempting, Webb suspected, to disguise stress.

"I gather from my son, Chief Inspector, that you felt he might know more than he told you about those letters and phone calls. However, we've now been over everything, and it's clear he was mistaken, so you needn't waste any more time on him."

"I appreciate your calling, Mrs. Jessel," Webb said drily, "but you'll understand I must pursue inquiries as I think fit. I'd like to hear about your discussion, though; perhaps you'd both come in to see me."

Her voice rose. "But it was precisely to avoid—"

"Yes, I realize that, but we need a statement from you anyway; I didn't want to bother you on Saturday. I'll be here all morning."

There was a pause. Then, letting him know that she wasn't doing him any favours, she said tightly, "All right. I'm coming in to Shillingham anyway, so I'll call in. But my son, of course, is at school."

"I can arrange to see him later," Webb said blandly.

Now that her first grief was over and her poise regained, her attractiveness was more evident. The smart little suit snugly fitted her slim, taut body, and was the exact blue of her eyes. She settled herself in the chair by Webb's desk, and Crombie, with a tactful murmur, left the room. Sally Pierce brought in two cups of coffee, and Webb noted that his visitor put hers on the edge of his desk. To conceal the shaking of her hands?

"Now," he said easily, "exactly what was it I was supposed to have thought?"

She flushed. "Lance said you questioned him very closely about the letters and phone calls. You—seemed to think he knew who was responsible."

"And did he?"

She shook her head. "That's just it. He had an idea, but he was wrong."

"Who did he think it was?"

Her cup rattled in its saucer and she hastily abandoned it. "Does it matter, since he was mistaken?"

"Yes, I think it does."

A pause. Then, not looking at him, "He thought it might have been Robert Kent. He—Mr. Kent, that is, hadn't a very high opinion of James."

"Was he a business colleague?"

"No."

"A social acquaintance, then?"

She bent her head, fiddling with the buttons of her jacket, and the soft grey wings of hair screened her face. "Actually they only met once."

"Perhaps," suggested Webb, employing his detective powers, "there was jealousy between them?"

Her head came up, her eyes, startled, met his and then dropped.

"Yes," she acknowledged softly.

"Mrs. Jessel, I've no wish to pry, but in a murder case, personal matters one would prefer to keep private have to be brought into the open." She nodded, still avoiding his eyes. "So will you tell me about Mr. Kent?"

"He's fairly new to the district," she said quietly. "We met at the tennis club."

Webb nodded encouragingly. "You told me you played."

"James was always busy, Chief Inspector. I told you that, too. It's no excuse for what happened, but it is the cause."

"You and Mr. Kent became lovers?"

She nodded. "Which is something I'll regret for the rest of my life."

"Why, Mrs. Jessel? Because of your husband's death?"

"And because he found out."

"Recently?"

"A week ago. He came home unexpectedly early."

And found them in bed together, Webb thought. Surprise, surprise. "How did he react?"

"There was a row, of course. But once it was over, he never referred to it again."

"But the row itself? What was his attitude towards Mr. Kent?"

"Utter contempt," she said quietly. "And he was right, I know that now. Robert behaved despicably. He gave no thought to what I was going through; all he cared about was that his wife shouldn't hear of it, in case he lost his job."

"You haven't seen him since?"

"No. And I hope I never do again."

"You say Mr. Kent was concerned about his job."

"His boss is a friend of his wife's father."

"Might he have taken steps to keep your husband quiet?"

"By murdering him, you mean?" She laughed suddenly, a shocking sound. "He wouldn't have the guts," she said.

"As a matter of interest, what kind of car does he drive?"

"A Vauxhall Cavalier, I think."

"Colour?"

"Silver grey."

Pity. The paint analysis had come through that morning: the car which had driven past Jessel's body was identified as a 1988 Renault 9.

"How did your son learn about Mr. Kent?"

"He also came home earlier than expected. Robert had parked up the road, and Lance saw him running towards the car clutching his clothes—James hadn't allowed him to finish dressing. It was obvious what had happened, and for some reason Lance leapt to the conclusion that it was Robert who'd been responsible for the phone calls and things."

"Had Lance mentioned seeing him?"

"Not until yesterday. I knew he was worried about something, but for a long time he wouldn't tell me what. It wasn't easy for me, either," she added frankly. "I thought at least I'd been spared the boys knowing about Robert."

Webb tapped his pen reflectively on his desk. "You seem very certain Mr. Kent couldn't have attacked your husband. But isn't it possible he was deeply humiliated by his attitude, and by being forced to walk up the main road in his underclothes?" It was just possible, he thought, unwilling to dismiss a possible suspect, that the blue Renault was innocent.

"But what would killing James have achieved? To be sure of secrecy, he'd have had to kill me, too."

"You weren't likely to make your affair public. Nor, as you've just proved, would you suspect him. In any case, we'll have to see Mr. Kent. Have you his address?"

"He lives in Lethbridge Drive, but I've never been to the house."

"We'll find it. Now you've had a chance to think, has anyone else occurred to you who might have wanted your husband dead?"

"Someone I know, you mean? But what about the April Rainers? Surely it was them?"

"You might know them under another name."

She looked startled. "Oh, I see. Well, like Lance, I thought at first it was Robert who'd made the phone calls, but when I mentioned it to him, he said not."

"You can forget the phone calls, Mrs. Jessel. And the car advertisement and the manure. They weren't connected with the murder."

"You know who was responsible?"

"Yes." He hesitated, but she had the right to know. "It

was a man called Fenshawe, husband of the ex-editor of Broadshire *Life*."

"Oh." She let out her breath in a long sigh. "Gaby Fenshawe's husband. Yes, that makes sense."

Webb said diffidently, "If you want a summons issued—" but she was shaking her head.

"No, of course not. They were a nuisance, nothing more, and I can understand why he did it."

"He also admits to sending the earlier letters, which just leaves the last one."

She said softly, " 'Evil deeds which assault and hurt the soul.' Oh, *James! Why* did you have to make so many enemies?" She reached blindly for a handkerchief.

"Drink your coffee," Webb said gently, as though she were a child, and, like one, she obediently lifted her cup. Then she paused, looking at him over its rim.

"You won't have to see Lance now, will you? He's been through enough, and it has nothing to do with James's death."

"He'll need to make a statement," Webb said, "but we'll go easy on him."

When she had gone, Nina Petrie tapped at the door. "We've had another call that seems genuine," she said. "From Chichester this time."

"Ye gods! We'll soon have covered the entire country. Would you ask Davis and Trent to take this one?"

"Yes, sir. Anything particular you want them to look for?"

"Yes," Webb said slowly. "We need to know if the victim's name had been in the papers shortly before he died, and—though it's difficult to ask the bereaved—whether the deceased had done anything at all reprehensible." "Evil deeds," he thought. For that matter, John Fletcher's "wrongdoing." He must arrange for him and his pals to be brought in for questioning.

Nina was still waiting at the door.

"When was this killing, did they say?"

"Last November."

"Contemporary newspaper reports might be helpful. God, Nina, who the devil are these April Rainers? And, heaven help us, are there really eight of them? With numbers like that, they really could cover the whole country. Still"—he pushed back his chair—"no use anticipating trouble. I'm going over to see the mob at Broadshire *Life*. Perhaps they can shed some light on all this."

The offices of the glossy magazine were very different from those of the Broadshire *News,* which Webb knew well. Thick carpet covered the floor, and far from the veil of cigarette smoke that assaulted any visitor who stepped over the threshold of the *News,* there wasn't even an ashtray in sight. Webb was duly thankful. He and Jackson approached the sophisticated young lady behind her designer desk.

"Chief Inspector Webb and Sergeant Jackson, Shillingham CID. We'd like to see whoever's in charge."

"I'm not sure—" she began automatically, and stopped at the look in Webb's eye. "One moment," she substituted, and pressed a button on the instrument in front of her.

The voice at the other end reached them clearly. "Jenny, I said—"

"It's the police, Mr. Peabody."

"Oh God. Well, only to be expected, I suppose." Jackson wondered if, like old-time servants, the police were supposed to be deaf. "Show them up, then."

The girl rose and came round the desk. Her skirt was short, her legs shapely and elegantly clad, her heels high. Jackson, reminding himself he was a married man, followed her and Webb over to the scrolled doors of a lift. They were borne upwards in silence, scarcely seeming to move. The doors glided open and a carpeted corridor stretched before them, with exotic plants spotlighted at intervals along it. Literally Renta-Plant, Jackson thought; bit different from Carrington Street. The girl stopped at a door halfway along the passage, knocked, opened it, and stood to one side. The two policemen passed inside.

More thick carpet and elegant furniture, and a wall of windows overlooking the park and sports centre. A short, self-important-looking man rose to greet them, glancing at his watch.

"Good morning, gentlemen. I'm sure you'll appreciate that things are extremely fraught this morning. The phone hasn't stopped ringing, and—"

"Our time is valuable, too, sir," Webb broke in. "We won't keep you longer than necessary."

"Yes, I see. Of course." A small white hand with a gold signet ring waved vaguely at a couple of chairs.

"We're completely stunned," Peabody added after a moment, when, following his usual practice, Webb didn't immediately speak. "Mr. Jessel was here on Friday afternoon. And now, three short days later—" He folded his hands on top of his desk, clasping them tightly as though to control himself. Then he looked expectantly at Webb.

"I believe there was a lot of resentment at the way the takeover was handled," Webb began.

Peabody bristled. "On the contrary, everything possible was done to smooth the transition. As you can see, no time was lost and no expense spared in improving working conditions." He gestured at the luxury around them. "We—"

"For instance," Webb continued smoothly, "in spite of the agreement with the previous owners, there were a number of redundancies."

"Forgive me, Chief Inspector, but I presume you have little experience of management. A concern such as ours can't afford to carry passengers. One has—"

"I don't wish to discuss business ethics, Mr. Peabody. I'm concerned only with who might have killed Mr. Jessel."

The man stared at him, and his eyes were suddenly alarmed. "You surely don't imagine that anyone connected—"

"I repeat, there was a lot of resentment. Have either you or, to your knowledge, Mr. Jessel ever received threats of any kind?"

Peabody's anxiety deepened. "Certainly not. You don't think—"

He never seemed to finish his sentences, Jackson noted. Not a good trait, surely, in a manager. Though to be fair, the governor wasn't giving him much chance to.

"What I think is immaterial, Mr. Peabody. I'm trying to establish who had a motive to kill your employer."

"But you can't imagine—I mean, surely he wasn't killed for business reasons?"

"What others would you suggest?"

Peabody was becoming noticeably more flustered. Possibly he saw himself as the next victim. "Well, I don't know, I'm sure. What are the usual motives? Money? Fear?"

"Revenge?" Webb suggested helpfully, and saw the man flinch. "Look, sir, I'm simply asking for your help. Was there anyone who had particular reason to resent Mr. Jessel?"

"No, of course not. Except, possibly, Gaby Fenshawe, and to give her her due, she took it very well."

"What about the man who died? Did any of his relatives approach the company?"

"Jessel Enterprises wasn't responsible for his death," Peabody said stiffly. "He had a weak heart. It was simply unfortunate that the attack came so soon after his—"

"Dismissal? Most unfortunate. But did anyone approach you? His widow, for instance, or someone representing her?"

"His wife had predeceased him, but there was some rather unpleasant correspondence with a son, I believe."

"That's the kind of thing I need. I'd be glad of his name and address, and also those of everyone here who lost their jobs when Jessel Enterprises took over." Though what any of them had to do with Ted Baxter was anyone's guess. He waited while Peabody lifted one of the phones on his desk and put through the request.

"Was your relationship with Mr. Jessel a purely business one?" he continued then.

"Yes; we never met outside office hours."

"So you knew little of his private life?"

"Nothing at all."

"Have you met his wife?"

"At official functions. A charming lady."

Routine questions followed, but Mr. Peabody had recovered his composure and nothing further was forthcoming. Jackson was glad when they were interrupted by a girl with the computer print-outs. She was darker than the receptionist, but equally beautiful and soignée. Must be nice to have someone like that to bring in your cuppa, he thought wistfully. Fair brighten your day. The governor was getting to his feet.

"Thank you very much, Mr. Peabody. And if anything else occurs to you, perhaps you'd get in touch. Now, could we have a word with your new editor?"

For a moment, Jackson thought Peabody was going to refuse. But he bit back his annoyance, and they were duly taken down more corridors to the editor's office.

Colin Campbell was a rangy young man with overlong dark hair and quick, intelligent eyes. From first impressions, Webb would have found it hard to choose between him and Gaby Fenshawe. Possibly in Jessel's eyes his maleness had been his chief advantage. From what he'd heard of Jessel, Webb had formed the impression that he wouldn't have taken women in business seriously. Decorative secretaries, fine, but speaking to them on equal terms, never.

"What was your immediate reaction on hearing of Mr. Jessel's death?" he asked the young man.

The bright eyes regarded him quizzically. "Sanitized version?"

"No, the truth."

"I thought, Hard luck, old chap, but you had it coming."

"Would you explain that reaction?"

Campbell shrugged. "There were times when I could have throttled him myself. And others when I'd happily have spent an entire evening with him over a couple of drinks, putting the world to rights. He could be a bastard, but he was excellent company."

"How did you feel about being appointed to this job?"

"Over Fenshawe, you mean? Not good, to be honest. I felt she'd been treated shabbily. But she'd lost it anyway, and if I turned it down, someone else would get it, so there was no point in making a grand gesture."

"Were you resented on her behalf?"

"Oh, certainly. I still am, particularly by the old guard, and I can't blame them." He met Webb's eyes. "You're not serious about this April Rainers rubbish?"

"Have you anything better to suggest?"

"Not offhand. But for a start, I don't see the connection between Jessel and that other chap, the wife-beater. That is, I don't *think* Jessel beat his missus."

"There are other motives for murder," Webb said mildly. "How long had you known Mr. Jessel?"

"About five years. I worked on one of his other publications."

But as with Peabody, further questioning produced nothing new. Colin Campbell could add no more names of potential suspects.

Their last interview of the day was with Robert Kent, and was held back till six o'clock to allow him time to return home.

Mike Romilly also lived in Lethbridge Drive, Webb reflected, thinking of the editor of the Broadshire *News* for the second time that day. He must contact Mike and hand over the latest batch of cartoons. It still amazed him that the paper not only paid him good money for his doodling, but constantly pestered him for more. Still, his flair for caricature had more than once helped solve a case for him, pinpointing weaknesses in the cartoon figures that only his subconscious had registered. If things hadn't moved forward in a day or two, he'd be getting out his easel again.

"Here we are, guv. Number twenty-two." Jackson drew up in front of an attractive, double-fronted semi. It was starting to get dark, and lights showed invitingly in the hall and left-hand window. Jackson wondered if Kent were watching them from one of the darkened rooms. Surely he must be expecting them? Or was he confident Mrs. J. wouldn't mention his name?

They got out of the warm car into the cool evening air. The sky above was clear, its deepening shadows cloudless. On a tree somewhere, a blackbird was singing its vespers. Jackson bent to unlatch the gate, and they walked together up the path.

Their ring was answered by a pleasant-faced young woman with a child in her arms. The little boy's face was smeared with chocolate.

"Mrs. Kent?"

"That's right."

"Is your husband home?"

"Yes, he's bathing our little girl. Can I take a message?" She looked at them doubtfully.

"We'd like a word with him, please. Shillingham CID."

She caught her breath, and the child she held whimpered and struggled to be put down. Her grip tightened protectively. "Is something wrong?"

How to answer that? Her marriage, if nothing more, could be in danger.

"We won't keep him long," Webb said evasively.

In silence she held the door wide and they stepped inside. The lighted room had cushions on the floor, and a teddy-bear lying half under a chair. "The children have just had their playtime," Mrs. Kent apologized, "and I haven't had time to tidy up. If you'll sit down, I'll get my husband."

Jackson's eyes followed her as she left the room, the child's rosy, chocolatey face watching him over her shoulder. At least Kent had had time to bath his daughter, he reflected, which was more than he'd do this evening.

Robert Kent arrived breathless, whether from anxiety or bathtime games, Webb couldn't be sure. He was tall and florid-complexioned, with dark eyes and a loose, womanizing mouth. A small nerve twitching in his cheek betrayed the nervousness he was striving to conceal.

"You wanted to see me?"

"Chief Inspector Webb, sir, Shillingham CID. And my colleague, Sergeant Jackson."

"Yes?"

"We'd like to know, sir, the last time you saw Mr. James Jessel."

The impact of the question took away what remained of Kent's breath, and he gasped as though struck in the solar-plexus. "Who?" he asked after a moment. It was a brave attempt.

Webb said smoothly. "You must have read of his death in the papers?"

Relief briefly flooded Kent's face. "Oh, I see. Yes, of course. But—why should you think I knew him?"

"Because of your relationship with his wife," Webb said brutally, destroying his hope stillborn.

Kent moved convulsively to the door and pushed it shut. "Look," he said in an urgent undertone, "I don't know what you've been told, or by whom, but you're entirely misinformed. I know Mrs. Jessel very slightly, since we belong to the same tennis club, but that's all."

"You're not being very helpful, Mr. Kent," Webb said reproachfully. "We know for a fact that a week last Saturday, Mr. Jessel came home to find you with his wife. Since it was

Mrs. Jessel herself who told us, I presume you're not going to bother denying it?"

"*Cynthia?*" exclaimed Kent incautiously. "But—I don't understand. Why should she mention my name?"

"Because her son thought you might have been making nuisance calls."

"But I didn't! I told her—" He broke off, and swallowed drily. "Look, all right, we did have a thing going, but it wasn't important. She was bored, her husband was a workaholic and she was looking for a bit of fun. That's all it was. But for God's sake don't let my wife hear about this. It was bad enough—" Again he stopped.

"Last time?" Webb finished for him, trying to keep the contempt out of his voice. The man flushed and looked away. What had Cynthia Jessel said, when he'd suggested Kent could have a motive for murder? "He wouldn't have the guts." He suspected she was right.

"Perhaps, Mr. Kent, having got all your denials out of the way, you'll now answer my question. When did you last see Mr. Jessel?"

Kent moistened his lips. "I only ever saw him once—on the day you mentioned."

"You didn't lie in wait for him on Friday evening with a nylon stocking in your hand?"

Kent's eyes widened in horror. "God, you don't think that? Why should I kill him? It would make more sense if he'd killed me."

"Because you were fearful of losing your job if the news got out?"

Kent shook his head violently. "I can see you haven't much of an opinion of me," he said jerkily. "Come to that, I haven't of myself. But I'm not a killer, Chief Inspector. That, I promise you. I haven't the stomach for it." A more acceptable paraphrase.

"Where were you on Friday night, sir?"

"Here. The last place I'd have gone to was the Jessels'. I was still expecting him to come after me, to tell the truth."

"Can you prove you were at home?"

"My wife will confirm it, if you're prepared to believe her."

"We'll check with her." He nodded to Jackson, who left the room. "In the meantime, I'd like you to accompany us back to the station for further questioning."

Kent blanched. "Why?"

"You've already lied to us, Mr. Kent. We want to be sure you're not still lying."

"But I swear—"

Webb raised a hand. "You can swear at the station. Now, when the sergeant's had a word with your wife, you can tell her what's happening. All being well, you should be home again in an hour or two."

And perhaps, Webb thought minutes later, as he and Jackson escorted the frightened man down the path, the brush with murder would have scared him out of any more amorous exploits, in which case some good may come out of the sorry business after all.

11

EARLIER THAT EVENING, after his last lesson, Mark had called on Felicity's former music teacher, Miss Grundy, who, he'd discovered, was living in sheltered accommodation only minutes from his own home.

Fernley Park was a custom-built complex, with some two dozen flats grouped round two courtyards, and, being in the centre of town, was in easy walking distance of shops, library, cinemas and the post office. Miss Grundy had one of the smaller flats on the ground floor, and was at her door to greet him.

"I saw you coming from my window," she told him. "That's one of the advantages of being at the front of the building, rather than tucked away round the back. There's always something to see on King Street, and I still feel part of the town. That's very important, now I can't get about as much."

She was a diminutive old lady with silver hair in a skimpy bun. She wore a dazzling white blouse with a high lace collar fastened with a cameo, and a black skirt reaching to her skinny ankles. Her gnarled hands were cruelly misshapen, and Mark remembered Felicity's speaking of the arthritis which had recently prevented letter-writing.

He followed her into the small, cosily furnished living-room. A photograph of Felicity held pride of place on the television set.

"I'm delighted you're doing her biography," Miss Grundy

said, following the direction of his eyes. "I can't imagine why she's staved off all requests until now."

"Actually, nothing definite's been settled. It would involve my taking a year or so off work if I went ahead with it."

She smiled. "And I gather you're a successor of mine, teaching music at Ashbourne?"

"That's right, yes. Did you go to the school concert?"

"Indeed I did, and to the première. Weren't they magnificent? That new concerto was quite breathtaking. And to think my little Felicity composed it! Of course, she was always one of my star pupils. Most children came to me at the age of seven or eight for their first music lessons, but by then Felicity was already a competent performer. In fact, she composed her first piece when she was only eight years old, and a charming little rondo it was."

"I believe her father was against her making a career of music?"

"Indeed yes. I had several very difficult interviews with him, pleading on her behalf, but he was an obstinate man and wouldn't give way. Now, Mr. Templeton, before we go any further and I'm carried away with nostalgia, what may I offer you to drink? Tea? Or would you prefer sherry?"

"Sherry would be very welcome, thank you." And probably easier for the poor old thing to produce, he thought.

"I was very much hoping Felicity would come and see me," Miss Grundy remarked as, holding the sherry bottle between her bent hands, she poured the liquid carefully into two glasses. "Still, I know she's very busy."

"She's here for another week yet," Mark told her, "and I know she's intending to visit you. She said so."

The old lady's face lit up. "That'll be something to look forward to."

"Did you gather she was happy at home? As a child, I mean?"

"Oh, I think so. Her mother and brother were both musi-

cal, but inevitably there was friction with her father. Sometimes I'd come into the music room to find her in tears."

"But she never thought of giving up?"

"Never. She was a very strong-willed little girl—and despite her small stature, she could be quite fierce! I'll never
forget her charging to the rescue of that large, plain child—
what was her name? Harriet something. Anyway, she was
being bullied by some fifth-formers, and Felicity flew into the
fray like a Yorkshire terrier nipping at the heels of elephants!
Oh yes, she'd plenty of courage, and it stood her in good
stead."

"And earned her the lifelong devotion of Hattie Matthews," Mark said with a smile. "She's now her secretary-
companion. Did you ever suspect, in those early days, that
Miss Harwood would become a world-famous composer and
violinist?"

The old lady smiled reminiscently. "It's easy to be wise
after the event, but you know, I rather think I did. As I told
you, she came to me as quite a competent little pianist, but I
had the thrill of giving her her first violin lesson, and I'll
never forget her face. It was—ecstatic. As you must know,
Mr. Templeton, teaching music can be a soul-destroying oc-
cupation, but a pupil like Felicity Harwood makes up for a
lifetime of uninterested, mediocre performers."

"Then I hope I'm lucky enough to find one!"

"So do I, but they're rare birds." She looked across at him.
"You say you're not sure you'll proceed with the biography?"

"Not yet. I'm having a dry run, to see how I get on."

"The point is, I have some very precious mementoes—her
early compositions and so on—which I've treasured all these
years. Were you to go ahead, I'd be prepared to loan them to
you. You seem a sensible young man, and I'm sure you'd take
care of them. After my death, they're destined for the British
Library."

Mark leant forward. "Couldn't I borrow them anyway?

Please? I've always been a great admirer of Miss Harwood, and it would be fascinating to see them. And if I decide against the book, I promise faithfully to bring them straight back to you."

"Very well, then. Her first piece is among them, so you realize how priceless they are. It was interesting, you know—I saw her being interviewed on television a few months ago, and they happened to ask her the title of her first composition. She couldn't remember; but I know, because I still have it. I must tell her when she comes."

She moved across to an old satinwood desk and unlocked the top drawer, taking out a bulky, dog-eared file stuffed with papers, which she put into his hands. "Guard them with your life. If anything happens to them while they're in your care, I'll come back and haunt you! But whether you go ahead or not, I hope you'll come and see me again. I've enjoyed our chat."

The early morning had been misty, but now the sun had broken through, lighting to flame the leaves which still clung tenaciously to the trees. Halted at the traffic-lights, Webb briefly felt the need to paint them. Then more urgent matters crushed the artist in him, and he ran through a mental checklist. The members of the commune had been collected in police cars and were now being interrogated. Redundant Broadshire *Life* staff were being traced and interviewed. Terence Denbigh's son had made a statement, but appeared to be in the clear. As for the reports from the previous cases—He glanced at Jackson beside him.

"Anything strike you about those reports, Ken?"

"Can't say it did. OK, so the letters and the MO are a link, plus the fact that none of the cases have been closed. But the victims were a mixed bag, weren't they?"

"Yes. I wish we could find a common denominator."

"You could reckon we've an advantage, in having two on our hands. At least we can compare them."

"And find they, too, have no common factor."

"Think it's one of those crusade cases, guv, like the 'Delilah' killings a few years back?"

"It's possible. But most serial murderers have a bee in their bonnet—in the 'Delilah' case, unfaithful wives—and as you say, these victims are all different: men of varying ages, women, even a fairly young lad up in Leeds, and from completely different backgrounds.* Yet if the notes our two received are typical—and we know the London one came into the same category—they're all accused of something—'crimes against humanity' and such high-faluting stuff. Granted, Baxter and Jessel had behaved badly in some respects, but they were hardly capital offences."

"They might be to someone with an outsize chip on his shoulder. Someone who'd been affected by their actions."

"But *who*, Ken? We keep coming back to that. Was there some connection we haven't spotted between Baxter and Jessel, involving a third person? Someone who upped and gave them both the chop? For instance, could Jessel once have employed Baxter in some capacity? Go back to the post office, would you, and ask to see his records. They'll have a note of previous employers. It's a long shot, but we can't afford to miss a trick on this one. I'll drop you off here. Meet me at the Brown Bear in an hour's time."

As Jackson set off up the road, Webb switched on the car radio to check the time. The last bleep of the twelve o'clock signal filled the car, followed immediately by the news headlines. He adjusted his watch and reached to switch off the news, having too many problems of his own to worry about international ones. But the announcer's voice knifed through his inattention and he froze, his hand on the radio knob.

"Concern is growing for the safety of the composer and violinist Felicity Harwood, who set off for Edinburgh early this morning in a private plane. She was due to receive the

* *A Shroud for Delilah*

Freedom of the City in a ceremony at the Usher Hall, but her plane is now overdue and there has been no contact with it since the pilot reported foggy conditions as he flew over the Lake District. Miss Harwood gave a world première of her latest composition, a violin concerto, in her home town of Shillingham last Saturday. It was widely acclaimed as a masterpiece."

Webb switched off the radio and the car was quiet, insulated from the normal life outside, where shoppers hurried to complete their purchases before the lunch-time closedown.

God, no! he thought convulsively. Only last night, he'd played the recording Hannah had made of Saturday's concert and been overwhelmed by the mastery of it. If anything happened to her now, at the height of her powers, what a tragic waste it would be.

He shook himself and started up the engine. It was too soon to mourn; the plane could have made a forced landing in an out-of-the-way spot, or simply flown off-course due to some faulty instrument. There were any number of possibilities, and one of them was bound to provide the answer.

After a subdued lunch with Jackson at the Brown Bear, Webb was back at his desk when a tap at the door brought DC Jones into the room.

"Sorry to bother you, guv, but I've got Pussy Barlow downstairs."

"Rather you than me, Alf." The little cat-burglar was a regular informer of Jones's, but in Webb's view the importance of any news he might impart had to be balanced against the unpleasantness of coming into contact with him. He exuded a peculiarly nauseating aroma which was apt to get into one's nostrils and linger for hours afterwards.

"He wants a word with you. Says he has some information."

"What sort of information?"

"To do with the night Baxter died."

Webb's eyes narrowed. "He's taken his time—that was thirteen days ago. All right, I'll come down."

Pussy was leaning nonchalantly against the window-sill when Webb and Jones reached the interview room, and his personal scent came to meet them. Webb nodded to the constable on the door, who thankfully withdrew.

"Now, Pussy, what's all this about?"

"Slow down a minute, Mr. Webb. We need to do a spot of bargaining, me and you."

"Bargaining? Look, if you're wasting my time—"

"No, no, governor, nothing like that. But I have to protect my interests, don't I? That's only right."

"And how," Webb asked heavily, "do your interests conflict with what you have to tell me?"

Pussy rubbed the side of his nose. "One or two other things happened that night, governor."

Jones said flatly, "That break-in, guv, in Rankin Road."

Webb's pulses quickened, but he merely commented, "And there we were, thinking you'd retired!"

"So I have, governor, in a manner of speaking. But every now and then, well—the urge comes over me." Pussy shook his head sadly.

"Well, I can make no promises, but we'll see what we can do. Caution him, Constable." Jones did so. "Now, what is it?"

Pussy hesitated. "I'll still get my fee?"

"Give me strength!" Webb snapped. "Yes, if your information leads to identification, you'll get your fee. Now for pity's sake get on with it, man! I'm trying to conduct a murder inquiry!"

"Yes, well, I saw two blokes, like, scarpering out of Rankin Close."

"What time was this?"

"About half eleven, I reckon."

"Can you describe them?"

Pussy shrugged. "One big, one small. Not more than a lad,

by the look of him. See, I had my hand on the gate when I heard running footsteps, and ducked down smartish. I had a quick shifty through the bars, which was when I seen 'em, but once they'd rounded the corner they was out of sight."

"You were in the garden opposite Rankin Close?"

The little man hesitated, then nodded. "Thought I'd got some opposition, to tell the truth, though they wasn't carrying nothing. Figured they might have been surprised on the job and run off empty-handed."

"What direction did they take?"

"Got in a car further down the road and zoomed off towards the High Street."

"Did you see the car?" Pussy shook his head. "And you hadn't noticed them going into the Close?" Another shake. "Or anyone else drive in?"

"Nah. I'd been in the house, see."

"So you didn't get a look at their faces?"

"Have a heart, governor! I was scared of bein' seen meself, crouching down there by the gate. I wasn't going to cross the road and peer at 'em, now was I?"

"And the car drove off in the other direction, which means it presumably came in from the Marlton road end."

"Well?" Pussy demanded after a moment, as Webb continued to stare, frowning, down at the floor. "Is it any help, or isn't it?"

Webb sighed. "At least there weren't eight of them!" he said.

For Mark, there was no softening of the blow. Having spent the day at St. Anne's School, he'd heard nothing of the missing plane, and by the time he returned home that evening, its wreckage had been found. Neither Felicity Harwood nor her pilot had survived the crash.

Numbed, he stood in the hallway, the evening paper with its ugly black headlines in his hand. The report of the crash was followed by a brief synopsis of last week's concerts and

then a full obituary, with the photograph which had appeared
on the programme displayed alongside. Irrationally, he felt a
surge of anger. Even while the paper had applauded Felicity's
return to Shillingham, that obituary had been on file, ready
for just such an eventuality. Ghouls! he thought incoherently.

He went through to the living-room, his thoughts stum-
bling to Camilla and the family. What must they be feeling?
And Hattie Matthews, who, but for her injured ankle, would
also have died? As, he thought with a sudden chill, would he
himself, had his full day's schedule not made the trip impossible.

With a groan, he sank into a chair and put his head in his
hands. No more music, ever, by Felicity Harwood, when
with her last composition she had touched on genius. It was
unbelievably cruel, impossible to accept. He raised his head,
and his eyes fell on the pile of cassettes. The biography! What
would happen now?

The sound of the doorbell roused him from his misery. His
five o'clock lesson! Hell! For a moment he considered cancel-
ling it, but then, rising to his feet, he went to open the door.
It would at least give him something else to think about, and
at the moment there was nothing he could do.

The long evening crawled by, and now Mark wished he had
other lessons to fill the empty hours. A heap of crumpled
paper bore evidence of his attempts at a letter of condolence,
and the stacked cassettes still lay at his elbow. He had only to
reach out and switch on the machine to hear Felicity's voice.
It was macabre, horrible.

With sudden clarity, he knew that he now had no option
but to go ahead with the biography, to carry out what could
be regarded as her dying wish. And as the realization came,
he also knew that he didn't want to, had subconsciously decided to withdraw. He was a musician, not a writer; delighting in the structure and artistry of her music, he was uninterested in the life of its composer. Yet because that love of her

work had brought him to her notice, he must give up a year of his life to research hers.

He ran his hand through his hair, fighting a sensation of being trapped. He should have known all along he couldn't do it, should have said so, firmly and at once. But he'd been flattered, and then there was Camilla. He accepted now that he'd delayed his refusal to allow himself more time with her. God, what a mess! What a tragic, tangled, inescapable mess!

The doorbell shrilled through the house, making him jump. Startled, he looked at the clock on the mantel. Nearly half-past ten. Who could be calling at this hour?

He went through to the hall, switched on the porch light, and opened the door. Camilla herself stood on the step. Mark stared at her blankly, unable to think of a word to say.

"I had to get out of the house," she said jerkily. "May I come in?"

"Of course. I'm sorry. God, Camilla—"

She brushed past him, not letting him finish his sentence, and went ahead of him into the living-room. "A large brandy wouldn't go amiss," she said.

He poured her one and handed it to her, noting her pallor with an aching, helpless compassion. She gulped half of it down. Then she said tremulously, "That's a bit better. Mother and Dad have flown up to Barrow. I stayed behind with Gran and Hattie."

"How—how are they?"

"I don't think Gran's taken it in. She's gone downhill very rapidly in the last week or so. But Hattie—" Camilla shuddered. "We had to send for a doctor to sedate her." She put her glass down quickly, and moved towards him. "Hold me, Mark."

His arms closed convulsively round her. "I keep wondering what it must have been like," she said into his shoulder. "Did she know they were going to crash, and if so, for how long?"

"Hush, darling." He could feel her trembling, and raised

her head gently, meeting her troubled eyes. Then, with a murmur which he didn't catch, she reached up, pulled his face down to hers, and started to kiss him.

Minutes later, Mark switched off the lights and they went hand-in-hand up the stairs.

12

"THE ACCIDENT INVESTIGATION TEAM think there may have been an explosion on board," Chief Superintendent Fleming was saying, "and at this stage, they haven't ruled out sabotage. Know of anyone who might have had it in for Miss Harwood, Spider?"

"It's hard to imagine, sir. She—" Webb broke off, remembering her unaccountable collapse at the concert and Hannah's voice telling him about it: "She'd a look of total shock, as though she'd seen someone or something she hadn't expected to see." God, was it possible—?

"What is it, man? Has something occurred to you?" The Chief Super's bird-like eyes were watching him intently.

"It's only a thought, sir, but it's just possible she received a note from the April Rainers."

"Merciful heavens, I hope not! We're getting enough stick, with no one arrested yet for the other two, without having a world-famous victim on our hands. What gave you that idea?"

Webb explained.

"And you think a note may have been hidden in one of the bouquets?"

Webb frowned. "That's what occurred to me, but I'm not sure it would wash. She'd hardly have had time to read it, would she? Anyway, the deputy headmistress went through the bouquets afterwards and could find nothing suspicious."

"Why should she do that?"

Too much time spent with me, Webb thought with grim humour. Aloud, he said, "She had the impression Miss Harwood received a shock when she glanced down at the flowers."

"Who handed up the bouquets?"

"I'm not sure. I imagine one of the music staff, but I can find out."

"What I'm getting at is if there were a death threat in one of them, it must have been inserted at the last minute. You wouldn't get a message like that via the local florist."

"Quite." Webb stood up. "If you'll excuse me, sir, I'll sort this out straight away and come back to you."

It was a long time since he'd called at the school. Webb drove up the winding drive past banks of evergreens and the deserted tennis courts and pulled up outside the front door. In the October sunshine, the Virginia creeper which clothed the front of the building glowed red and gold. Allowing himself no time to appreciate it, he rang the bell. Through the glass door he saw a woman who was crossing the hall hesitate, glance towards him, and then come to open it.

"Can I help you?"

"I'd like a word with Miss James, please. Chief Inspector Webb, Shillingham CID."

The woman's eyes widened. "If you'll come inside, Chief Inspector, I'll try to find her for you."

He waited in the hall, feeling large and conspicuous as a group of small girls clattered down the staircase en route to another classroom, each glancing curiously at him as she passed.

Hannah's voice said, "Chief Inspector Webb? I believe you wanted to see me."

"I'd be grateful if you could spare me a couple of minutes. There are some questions I'd like to ask about the school concert."

"Of course. The whole school is stunned by the accident."

She led the way to her study. It was as pleasant as her sitting-room at home, though considerably smaller. In a chair by the window, basking in the sunshine, lay the small ginger kitten.

Hannah closed the door behind them and turned to face him. "What is it, David? What's happened?"

"In view of what you told me about Miss Harwood's collapse, I'm wondering if there's any connection with the April Rainers."

Hannah paled, staring at him. "But—but how? You surely don't mean the plane crash wasn't an accident?"

"It's possible. There might have been an explosion when it was still in the air. Look, love, it's only an idea and there are a lot of points against it. Such as, could she have had time to read a note before fainting? And if she did, what happened to it, since you didn't find it? Then again, the concert was six, not eight, days before the crash. And finally, why should people with an MO involving nylon stockings suddenly switch to a bomb? If, in fact, there *was* a bomb."

Hannah moistened her lips. "So how can I help you?"

"I'd like to know how the bouquets were dealt with. What time they started to arrive, where they were put until the end of the concert, who could have had access to them, and so on."

"I'll phone for the secretary." Hannah sat down behind her desk, and the kitten jumped from its chair and up onto her knee. "Could you come in for a moment, Miss Hanson?"

They waited in silence, Hannah's fingers absentmindedly caressing the kitten's ears. There was a knock on the door, and the woman who had admitted Webb came into the room, an apprehensive look on her face.

"Yes, Miss James?"

"Miss Hanson, the Chief Inspector is anxious to know whether anyone might have had the opportunity to interfere with Miss Harwood's bouquets during the concert. Were you in charge of them?"

"I took some of them in, yes."

"What time did the first one arrive?" Webb asked.

"Early afternoon, I'd say. I know it was after lunch, because I put them in the pantry, where it was cool, and all the lunch things had been cleared away."

"And each time a delivery was made, you carried them through?"

"Well, I took in several, but I left a message with the caretaker that all the flowers were to be taken to the pantry."

"How is the pantry approached?"

Hannah rose, tipping the kitten to the floor. "Would you like to see it?"

The three of them walked along a checker-tiled corridor past large double doors leading to the dining-hall. At the end of the passage were the kitchens, and just short of them, on the right-hand side, the cool, stone-floored pantry. A large stone sink stood in one corner and Miss Hanson waved towards it with a flustered hand. "I put them there. Either standing in the sink or, when it was full, resting on the draining-board."

"There were a lot of bouquets?"

"A couple of dozen, I'd say."

"Would anyone normally come in here once school dinner was over?"

"Not until the boarders' supper-time."

"Is there any other access apart from the way we came?"

"Through the kitchen." Hannah nodded at a communicating door.

"Would anyone have been in there?"

"Yes. We'd invited about a dozen guests, including the Harwoods, for cocktails before the concert. The canapés and so on were prepared during the afternoon."

"One last question: who retrieved the flowers from here and took them into the hall?"

"A team of senior girls, led by Miss Maybury, head of Music."

Webb sighed. He wasn't much farther forward. "Well, thank you for your help, ladies. That's all for the moment."

Hannah walked back to the front door with him. "What'll you do now?"

"Go and see the Harwoods, which won't be easy. They live just up the road, don't they, in Hampton Rise?"

"That's right, Fauconberg House. Their garden actually backs onto ours."

"Very convenient. However, since I'll want a woman officer with me, I'll have to go and collect her first."

Hannah said in a low voice, "I couldn't bear it if Miss Harwood came to harm through performing here. Will you call in when you get home, and tell me the latest?"

"I don't know what time it'll be."

"Whenever. I shan't sleep till I know."

"All right. See you then."

He got into the car and, without looking back, drove towards the gate, his mind already on the difficult interview ahead.

Sir Julian and Lady Harwood had just arrived back from Barrow when Webb and Nina called. They were still shaken and disorientated, and didn't at first appreciate the significance of the police visit.

"But I don't understand," Sir Julian repeated patiently. "How can my sister's death be of interest to you, Chief Inspector?"

"The cause of the crash hasn't been identified yet, sir," Webb said diplomatically. "In the meantime, we're trying to go over the last week or so of Miss Harwood's life, looking for any unusual occurrences."

Lady Harwood frowned. "What sort of occurrences?"

"For instance, I believe she was taken ill at the Ashbourne School concert?"

Sir Julian made a dismissive gesture. "It was the heat and excitement, that's all."

Hannah had told him the first thing she'd said as she came round was "Hattie." Perhaps she, whoever she was, would be in a position to help him. He began tentatively, "I understand Miss Harwood's friend is staying here?"

"Miss Matthews, you mean? Yes; but for a broken ankle, she'd have been on the flight with my sister. She's extremely distressed, as you can imagine."

"Nevertheless," Webb said gently, "it's imperative that we should speak to her."

"Out of the question!" said Sir Julian at once, but his wife lifted her hand.

"Just a moment, dear." She turned to Webb. "It really is vital that you see her at once?"

"Yes, Lady Harwood, I'm afraid so. But if you'd prefer, Inspector Petrie here could interview her. That might be easier for her."

"Thank you, yes, I think it would. I'll take you up myself, Inspector."

As they left the room, Webb turned back to Sir Julian. "I believe your sister had commissioned a biography?"

"Not exactly; she asked Mr. Templeton if he'd do it, but he hadn't committed himself."

"Wasn't he rather a curious choice? He's not a writer, after all."

"He's a critic, Chief Inspector, and a very erudite one. Felicity valued his reviews enormously. Also, he's a devoted admirer. He's attended all the concerts she's given in this country over the last ten years or so. I can think of no one better qualified to evaluate her work."

Not totally convinced, Webb felt it politic to change the subject. "Had your sister to your knowledge received any threatening letters?"

"Good heavens, no. Threatening what?"

"Death, Sir Julian."

The man stared at him. "Are you serious?"

"Extremely."

"So that's what you meant about 'unusual occurrences,' "
he said slowly.

"I'm afraid so."

Sir Julian stared at the floor with furrowed brow, then
looked up again to meet Webb's eyes. "Well, I'm sorry, Chief
Inspector. My sister certainly never mentioned anything to
me, so I'm afraid I can't help you."

Webb could only hope that Nina was having better luck.

"You must understand," Lady Harwood had said as Nina
accompanied her from the room, "that Felicity and Miss Matthews were lifelong friends. She is as shattered as we are by
what has happened. I should also warn you that she's been
sedated, and her answers might not be as clear as you'd
wish."

Nina nodded. "I'll go as gently as I can."

They had come up the stairs and halted at one of the handsome oak doors on the landing. Lady Harwood tapped and
went inside. "Hattie dear, the police would like a brief word
with you. It won't take long." She nodded encouragingly at
Nina and withdrew, closing the door behind her.

The curtains were half-drawn across the window, shielding
the woman who sat there from the sunshine. She was a large
and ungainly figure swathed in a blue woolen dressing-gown,
and her heavily plastered foot was resting on a stool. As
Nina's eyes became accustomed to the gloom, she took in the
short, untidy hair, the heavy face puffed and swollen with
grief, the lack-lustre eyes. She advanced slowly towards her
and perched on the end of the bed.

"I'm Inspector Petrie, Miss Matthews. I'm sorry to trouble
you at such a time, but we do need your help."

The woman gazed at her stolidly without replying.

"I believe Miss Harwood was taken ill at the end of her
first concert here?"

Something flickered in the dull, stone-like eyes. At least

she was getting through. "Something frightened her, didn't it? As she came round, she asked for you."

A spasm contorted the heavy face and the woman caught her lip savagely between her teeth. "You see," Nina continued gently, "we don't know yet what caused the plane crash, and we're anxious to find out if Miss Harwood had received any kind of threats."

A look of total incomprehension met her. She went on carefully, "What frightened her, Miss Matthews? Was it something in one of the bouquets that were handed up to her? Something that might have some bearing on her death?"

The silence was unremitting. Nina was just wondering whether the sedation had blotted out all understanding when the woman spoke for the first time.

"You're asking if something in the flowers frightened Flick?"

Thank heaven, a response at last! "That's right. You were among the first to reach her. Do you think it's possible?"

There was another long silence. Then Miss Matthews said dully, "How did you guess?"

Nina felt a spurt of triumph. "There was? That was why she fainted?" A nod. She leant forward. "What was it, Miss Matthews? Did you see it yourself?"

The woman hesitated again, and Nina tried to curb her impatience. Then the words came slowly. "It was a card with a skull and crossbones on it. It was that which caught her attention. And it said, 'The next flowers you receive will be on your grave.'"

Nina's knuckles tightened on the edge of the bed. "Anything else you can remember?"

"It was written in green copperplate and signed 'The April Rainers.'"

Nina drew a deep breath. There were variations from the usual form, but it sounded genuine. "What happened to it, Miss Matthews?"

"It had fallen out of the bouquet and was lying by her

hand. No one else had noticed it, so I picked it up. After I'd read it, I destroyed it."

"Had you any idea who might have sent it?"

She shrugged. "There are always bitter, envious people who want to destroy the successful." She looked at Nina in bewilderment. "You're not taking it seriously, are you?"

"Haven't you heard of the April Rainers? There's been a lot about them in the papers." From the continuing blankness, apparently not. Unwilling to embark on a long explanation, she said instead, "Did you by any chance keep a note of the people who'd sent bouquets?"

"Yes." Miss Matthews wrenched her mind back from its own preoccupations. "Felicity liked a record of the names."

"Have you still got it?"

"It'll be on my desk."

"May I look?"

"If you like. It's headed Ashbourne School and the date. It'll be underneath the public concert list."

Nina opened the file lying on the desk. Sure enough, the top sheet of paper listed the flowers received at last Saturday's concert. Below it lay those sent to the school. "May I borrow this?"

"You can keep it, for all I care. Felicity won't need it again." And suddenly, appallingly, she began to weep, making no attempt to cover her face, sitting there with open, pain-filled mouth and streaming eyes.

Nina said, "I'm sorry to have upset you, Miss Matthews, but we're most grateful for your help. I'll go and get Lady Harwood."

Back at his desk, Webb flicked through the names of the flower-senders. Though no longer relevant, since the card that concerned them had been destroyed, the list provided a comprehensive rollcall of Shillingham's most distinguished citizens, from the mayor and mayoress, the Harwood family and several school governors—including, Webb noted sourly, Charles Frobisher—to big names in the commercial field, such as James Jessel.

He looked across at Nina. "What did you say the wording was, exactly?"

" 'The next flowers you receive will be on your grave.' But they weren't; she had another lot on Saturday. I saw the list."

"Still, it was close enough for jazz. But if we accept this was a genuine April Rainers message, why was it so different from the rest?"

"So it could be read at a glance?"

"But to what purpose? They couldn't have counted on her reading it on stage—it was a sheer fluke that she did."

"The skull and crossbones caught her eye, apparently."

"That could well be," Webb conceded. "The wonder is that it didn't catch anyone else's—the music teacher, or the girls who'd carried it through to the hall. But we come back to the fact that it's a completely different technique. No accusations either, you notice, and no time-limit."

"Perhaps they weren't sure they could get at the plane."

"But damn it, if they were so set on killing her, why not the usual method? That's what I don't understand." He tapped his pen on the desk. "You say this Hattie woman didn't seem to have heard of the April Rainers?"

"It's hard to tell. She didn't react in any way, but then she was responding slowly to everything, because of the sedation. Also, don't forget, when she read the note on Wednesday evening, there'd been no publicity, so the name wouldn't have meant anything."

"There's been plenty since."

"Yes, but she's a visitor here and mightn't read the local paper. And she's been laid up with her broken ankle, so could have missed the TV coverage."

"I asked Sir Julian if he knew of any threats to his sister, but he said no. She wouldn't want to worry the family, but she must have discussed it with Miss Matthews."

"They couldn't have come up with anything; all she said was that famous people make enemies."

"But some casual comment might have been made, which didn't seem important—about someone who'd been offended, or behaved strangely or something."

"Then we'll have to wait for the shock and sedation to wear off. She's not likely to have total recall at this stage."

Webb swore softly. "And I doubt if there was anyone else close enough—" He slammed his hand on the desk. "Of course! We might be in luck; Miss Harwood had asked someone at the school to write her biography. One of the music staff—Temple, or something. It seems he's had several sessions with her, asking questions into a tape-recorder. There's just a chance he could have picked up something. Go to the school, would you, Nina—I've already been up there today. Take Harry Sage with you, and see what you can glean."

Once again, the Broadshire *News* had a spectacular headline. DID APRIL RAINERS DOWN COMPOSER'S PLANE? And, beneath it, in only slightly smaller letters: "Was Felicity Harwood the latest victim of Shillingham's mafiosi? This is the question that is exercising the minds of police and accident investigation experts as speculation grows that the aircraft carrying the composer-violinist to Edinburgh was brought down deliberately. Meanwhile, it has been announced that a memorial service for Miss Harwood is to be held at Westminster Abbey in ten days' time."

The paper was lying on Hannah's sofa when, at eleven o'clock that evening, Webb finally reached her flat.

"You can ignore ninety percent of that," he commented, as he settled himself next to it and took the glass she handed him. "They've ruled out sabotage—the news has just come through. It was an engine fault that caused the crash."

"Well, it doesn't bring her back to life, but I'm glad it wasn't deliberate," Hannah said.

"As it happens, she might have died soon anyway." He

told her about the visit to Fauconberg House and the card with the skull and crossbones.

Hannah stared at him aghast. "You mean the murderer was there, in school, tampering with the bouquets?"

"It seems someone was. Unless he handed the flowers in at the door with the card already in place."

"Which isn't much better."

"I'm not happy about that card, Hannah. There's something odd about it, particularly since the plane crash was an accident after all. Why the change of routine? Why not a letter through the post, with specific accusations and a time-limit of eight days?"

"You think that's significant?"

"Yes, but I can't put my finger on why."

Hannah gazed thoughtfully into her glass. "I hear you sent someone to speak to Mark?"

"The biographer? Yes; he loaned us his cassettes, but at first run-through there's nothing startling. It was a long-shot anyway."

"So you're no nearer tracking down who these people are?"

"We've an eye-witness report, for what it's worth. Two men were glimpsed running out of Rankin Close at the time of the murder, but other than that one was tall and one short, there's no description. Dawson went back to the pub where Baxter'd spent the evening, to see if any of the clientele fitted that description, but all the landlord said was, 'Everyone's either tall or short, mate,' which didn't get us very far!"

"You've no other ideas?"

"I wouldn't say that. There's the odd bunch on Chedbury Common, for a start. Nothing's come to light under interrogation, but they're a weird lot and we're keeping them under surveillance."

"What about the murders in other parts of the country?"

"Our lads went to interview the local officers, but not

much has come up. Still, tomorrow's another day. On which note, I must drink up and let you get to your bed."

"You're not staying?"

"Daren't risk it, love. A phone call might come through at any time, and I have to be available."

"Sweet dreams, then, and let me know if there's anything else I can do."

13

THE OFFICERS who'd gone to check on the Chichester murder had now returned, and their report was on Webb's desk.

"Any help?" Alan Crombie inquired, when at last he raised his head.

"Nope—same rundown as the others. The victim had had some unpleasant publicity, though nothing serious. He received a letter giving the eight-day deadline, and was asphyxiated on the appointed day, probably by a nylon stocking. And despite intensive investigations, West Sussex came up with damn-all, which is par for the course."

Crombie sucked his teeth. "So what do we do now?"

"Feed the gen into the computer and see what it comes up with."

Crombie checked his watch. "I'll have to leave you to it. I'm due at court."

Webb nodded absentmindedly. Picking up his pen, he jotted down the list of towns that the April Rainers had visited: London, Cardiff, Liverpool, Leeds, Chichester.

He and Hannah had spent a pleasant weekend in Chichester a couple of years back, he reflected; they'd gone— His thoughts skidded to a halt, and he went rapidly through the list again. Then he sat for several minutes staring into space. It was impossible, surely, but every avenue had to be explored.

With a relieved glance at Crombie's deserted desk, he pulled the phone towards him and dialled Hannah's number.

Lady Harwood rose as Webb and Jackson were shown into the drawing-room. "I confess I'm surprised to see you again, Chief Inspector. Now that the cause of the accident has been established—"

Webb glanced at the girl who sat silently by the fire, and Lady Harwood said quickly, "I'm sorry, I don't believe you've met my daughter. Chief Inspector Webb, dear."

Webb nodded. "Miss Harwood." He turned back to her mother. "Yes, I apologize for troubling you again. But even though the crash was an accident, your sister-in-law had received a death threat."

Lady Harwood looked startled. "I didn't know that."

"We'd suspected something like that might have caused her collapse, and Miss Matthews confirmed it."

"You mean Felicity took it seriously?"

"I don't know, Lady Harwood, but it must have given her a shock. It was signed by 'The April Rainers.'"

The girl looked up. "The people who killed Mr. Jessel and that other man?"

"That's right, miss. We're hoping Miss Harwood might have said something that could give us a lead."

Lady Harwood still looked bewildered. "But why should anyone want to kill Felicity?"

Webb shrugged. "She said herself that if you're rich and famous, you make enemies."

"People who are spiteful and jealous, perhaps. But to think of *killing* her—that's entirely different." She shuddered.

"I presume your husband's out, ma'am?"

"Yes, he's—making arrangements for the funeral."

"And Miss Matthews—is she feeling any better?"

"She's a little calmer, thank you; but if you want to see her again, I'd be grateful if you could wait a while longer. She was very distressed after the inspector's visit."

At this stage he didn't feel justified in insisting. In any case, as Nina'd said, her mind was probably still clouded. But he needed to know exactly what Felicity Harwood had said about that note. He'd a nagging feeling it could be crucial.

"About the proposed biography," he began instead, and noted the girl's momentary tensing, "I believe Miss Harwood spent some time with this young man during the past week. Might she have confided in him, do you think?"

It was the girl who answered. "If you mean about the note, no, I'm sure she didn't. Mark would have told me."

"Unless," Webb suggested, "your aunt asked him not to?"

"He'd have told me when she died."

"Do you know of anyone, miss, who particularly disliked or resented her?"

"No." She paused, then added hesitantly, "I loved my aunt, Chief Inspector, but I'm aware that not everyone did. She could be dictatorial, especially where her music was concerned, and even my father had stormy rehearsals with her. I remember his saying more than once that the lead violinist had walked off the stage."

"Really, Camilla," Lady Harwood murmured, "I don't think we need go into that."

"On the contrary, ma'am, that's just the kind of thing we need, if we're to get to the bottom of this." Webb turned back to the girl. "So if she did have enemies, they were likely to be musicians?"

Camilla looked startled. "I didn't mean that."

"But they were the people she was most in contact with?"

"I suppose so, yes. But please don't think she was always difficult; she could be very patient and understanding."

"Did she receive a lot of mail, do you know?"

"I believe so. Hattie dealt with it."

"I wondered if there'd been other anonymous letters."

"Only Hattie could tell you that." And he wasn't able to ask her.

He thought for a moment, then tried another tack. "Was Miss Harwood ever married?"

"No."

"Did she have any romantic involvements that could have led to resentment or hatred—a rejected lover, for instance?"

"There were several men interested in her when she was younger," Lady Harwood replied, "but I hardly think any of them would have carried a torch this long."

"Except that they haven't been allowed to forget her, as would normally be the case. Her name was often in the news, and she appeared on television."

"True, but from what I remember, there'd been no bitterness."

Webb stood up. "I won't take up any more of your time. Thank you both for your help."

As they drove out of the gateway, he said suddenly, "We'll go back to my place, Ken. I want to play through those tapes again, and I'd like you to listen to them. You might pick up something I missed."

They turned out of Hampton Rise, drove a few yards down the hill, and turned left into Hillcrest, where Webb's block of flats stood.

There was a mid-morning atmosphere about the place which was alien to Webb. He felt an intruder, someone from a different time-zone. They went up in the lift in silence, and while he made two mugs of coffee, Jackson stood at the window, staring down the hill to the town at its foot.

"Gets everything into perspective, doesn't it," he commented, taking the mug offered; "seeing things at this distance."

"Yes, I unwind at that window when I come home each evening. Now, Ken, I'm going to switch this thing on. Like me, you only met Miss Harwood briefly. I'd like to know what impression you form of her after listening to this."

The two men settled themselves comfortably. Then Webb flicked the machine, and into the quiet room came Mark

Templeton's first, hesitant question: "Were you born in this house?"

Felicity's voice was low and husky as he remembered, telling of her childhood, her mother's encouragement of her music, her father's impatience with it. Diaries were mentioned; Webb made a note to ask Mark Templeton for them, though she might not have kept one in recent years.

She had recorded one of the tapes alone, apparently talking into it in free moments, and without the discipline of the interviewer's questions, the result was less structured. At one point, a knock sounded and a distant voice called. Felicity, close to the machine, replied, "Lord, is that the time? All right, Hattie, I'm coming." And a click ended the session.

"This is the most interesting from our point of view," Webb said, changing the cassette. The two men listened intently as Felicity recounted brushes she'd had with various people, and comments on the inefficiency or stupidity of others, wellknown names among them. "I've never pretended to be all sweetness and light," she told her interviewer.

"And she wasn't," Jackson agreed as the tape ended. "I can imagine she got a lot of backs up, though it was all fairly petty. Certainly not worth murdering for."

"Now there, Ken," Webb said slowly, "you have put your finger on it. In all seven April Rainers killings, the only one with any kind of motive was Baxter's, and even that's debatable. OK, he beat up his wife and she killed herself, but surely that's only motive for someone who was fond of her, and they're all in the clear.

"Then there's Jessel; he was a bastard, and that diarist bloke died after getting the sack, but it could be argued that was coincidence. It certainly didn't warrant the death sentence. And it was the same with the other cases. The victims were mean, or shady, or downright unpleasant, from the reports I read, but in no single instance did something stand out that would make a good, old-fashioned motive for murder."

"But that came over in the letters, didn't it, guv? They were pretty vague too, going on about anguish and hardship and hurting the soul and that. I'm putting my money on those weirdos at Chedbury. It seems right up their street, and whatever they say, they were in the same area as Baxter just before he died."

"You could be right. Well, we've spent enough time on this lot. We'll have a pie and a pint at the Brown Bear and see what inspiration that gives us."

At five o'clock, Hannah rang back with the information Webb had requested. He listened to it in silence, said simply, "Thanks. I'll be in touch," and hung up.

"What's the matter?" Crombie asked. "Did all your rabbits die?"

Webb looked across at him. "Know anything about the laws of coincidence, Alan?"

"Not a lot," confessed Crombie with a grin.

"Then I reckon you'd better start brushing up on them," Webb said, and, rising abruptly, walked out of the room, leaving the Inspector staring after him.

He was striding through the foyer when the Desk Sergeant stopped him. "Excuse me, sir, we're getting a message about a blue Renault."

"Yes?"

"One's been spotted in East Parade, driven by a young lady. Right year, Ted Finch says. He's tailing it at a discreet distance and requests instructions."

"Tell him not to intercept unless it leaves town. If we can trace it to an address, so much the better. Keep me informed."

Oakacre, where Mark Templeton lived, was only five minutes' walk from DHQ, and Webb set off on foot. Already the afternoon was dimming and street lamps flickered into life like Jaffa oranges. It was getting cooler, too. At the end of the week the clocks would go back, and winter would spring suddenly closer.

Webb passed County Court and turned into Fenton Road. He could remember when it lay on the edge of town, with the Library Gardens on its right and a rough common to the left. The gardens were still there, thank God, but the common where as a boy he'd played football had disappeared. Fronting Fenton Road were office blocks, estate agents' windows, building societies; and now the rot was spreading backwards, gradually eating up what had been open land.

The latest encroachment was Oakacre. He'd read about the development, but had no interest in seeing what he regarded as further despoilment. Now, business was taking him there. Ostensibly he was returning the cassettes, but his main purpose was to learn more about Felicity Harwood, and whether she had said anything significant when the tape wasn't running.

He reached the road sign and turned into the approach leading to the new estate. Parts of it were still little more than a building site, and on his right, what would eventually be a parade of shops was just beginning to take shape. Webb paused for a moment and stood with narrowed eyes, searching the muddy earth and heaps of builders' rubble for anything that might remain of his childhood playground. Then, with a sigh, he made his way over a strategically placed plank to Mark Templeton's front door.

His knock was answered after several minutes by a middle-aged woman in an apron. Faintly, he could hear the wavering, uncertain whining of a violin.

"I'm sorry, sir, Mr. Templeton has private lessons Thursday evenings," she said, when he stated his business.

"Until what time?"

"Well now, you're in luck there. Normally they go on till seven, but the six o'clock lesson's cancelled—sore throat or something. If you'd like to wait, he could see you in about twenty minutes."

Webb hesitated, frustrated by the delay. But he had come to see Templeton and had no intention of leaving without doing so. If he had to wait, so be it.

"Would you like a cup of tea, sir?" the woman asked, showing him into a room looking over the back garden. "It shouldn't be too noisy in here; the music room's sound-proofed, and I've finished my Hoovering. Just as well—Mr. T. says I should get a silencer!"

"A cup of tea would be welcome, thank you."

Alone in the room, Webb looked first, as always, at the pictures on the walls. A couple of prints only, but good mod-ern ones. The bookcase indicated a catholic taste, with some battered, well-read volumes among them, but it was the shelves beside the window that proved most interesting. In boxes, record sleeves, cassettes and compact discs were dis-played what must surely be the complete works of Felicity Harwood.

A voice behind him interrupted his inspection. "If you'd like to put one on, sir, I'm sure Mr. Templeton wouldn't mind."

"You're sure?"

"Oh yes, sir. Specially if you choose Miss Harwood's mu-sic." Her eyes filled with ready tears. "A tragedy that was, sir, and no mistake."

"Yes indeed," said Webb awkwardly. He selected a cas-sette at random, put it on the machine, and settled himself into one of the deep armchairs. There was no doubt about it, he thought, the music was superb. Having drunk his tea, he leant back, closing his eyes and giving himself up to the yearning, haunting sound of the violin. Yehudi Menuhin, it had said on the label—clear indication of the respect in which fellow musicians held the composer.

So immersed was he that he didn't hear Mark Templeton come into the room. The sound of the closing door alerted him, and he got hastily to his feet. The man who stood there was tall and good-looking, the strong brows and small cleft in

the chin reminding Webb of the young Laurence Olivier. He
came forward and held out his hand.

"I'm sorry to keep you waiting, Chief Inspector. I didn't
know you were here—Mrs. Bunwell has instructions not to
interrupt the lessons."

"I've been well entertained."

"Yes." Mark sobered. "I can't believe she's gone."

"I'm grateful for the loan of your interview tapes." He
indicated the stack he had placed on the low table. "Unfortunately we didn't get as much as we'd hoped from them."

"Do sit down. What were you looking for, exactly?"

Webb glanced across at him. "Did you know Miss Harwood had received a note from the April Rainers?"

"Camilla—Miss Harwood's niece, phoned at lunch-time. I
could hardly believe it."

"What did you think had caused her collapse?"

"I'd no idea. One moment she was smiling and bowing,
the next her face froze, turned deathly pale, and down she
went."

"I was hoping she might have mentioned the note outside
the recording session."

"Afraid not; she just said she was overcome by the heat
and excitement. I was one of the first to reach her, with my
father, who's a doctor and was in the audience."

"And what was his diagnosis?"

Mark shrugged. "A simple faint. And she made a remark-
ably quick recovery, according to the family."

"I was interested in the mention of diaries on the tape.
Have you had the chance to look at them?"

"Only one so far. Out of curiosity, I looked up the entry
for the day her father died."

"How old was she?"

"Fifteen."

"What did he die of?"

"He was killed in a train crash. But though it sounds hard,
it might have been just as well, because he wasn't prepared to

let her study music. It was only after his death that she was able to take it up seriously."

"An ill wind, perhaps. How long did she continue keeping a diary?"

"Until about halfway through her time at the Paris Conservatoire."

"They probably wouldn't be much help then."

"Not unless they revealed some lifelong enemy. But if it *was* the April Rainers, what connection could they have with her?"

"That's what we'd like to know. And with Baxter and Jessel, for that matter. Presumably you've interviewed Miss Matthews?"

"Actually, I haven't. There just hasn't been time; every spare moment was spent with Felicity herself. And to tell you the truth"—he grinned, looking suddenly boyish—"she rather frightens me!"

"Really? I've never met her."

"Oh, she's a formidable lady. The dragon at the gate."

Not much of the dragon about the distraught woman Nina had described, Webb reflected. "What about the old music teacher? Miss Grundy, was it?"

Mark's face sobered. "I'd forgotten about her, poor old thing. She idolized Felicity, and was looking forward to her calling round when she got back from Scotland."

"There was something on the tape about precious manuscripts."

"That's right. I locked them away and haven't got round to looking at them yet."

"Is it possible any old letters could have got caught up with them? I realize I'm grasping at straws."

"Well, let's see, shall we?"

Mark took out his keyring and, going over to one of the units, extracted a battered-looking file. He put it on the dining table and Webb went over to join him. The outside of the file was filmed with dust. Inside were stuffed music sheets, exercise books, a few photographs, and a large envelope inscribed "Felicity Harwood's First Composition!"

Webb straightened, watching as Mark picked up the envelope and withdrew the sheets inside it. "We're not likely to find any April Rainers here," he commented. And froze. Printed in childish capitals at the top of the music sheet was the title of the piece—APRIL RAIN.

Mark was the first to speak, and his voice shook. "Of all the abominable coincidences!"

"If it *is* a coincidence."

"What the hell do you mean?"

Webb said slowly, "I have a feeling she didn't receive a death threat after all."

"Then why did she faint, for Pete's sake?"

"I can hazard a guess." He reached for the manuscript, but Mark backed away.

"Oh no, you're not having this. I only lent you the tapes because the woman detective said they might hold a clue to the plane crash. If you think I'm going to stand by while you look for something sinister in a child's piece of music—God, it's unbelievable! Whatever theories you're hatching, you get no more help from me."

"I know how you feel," Webb said gently. "I'm very sorry."

"You've no *conception* of how I feel," Mark contradicted hotly. "Felicity Harwood is one of the world's great composers, and I'm not going to have aspersions cast at her when she can no longer defend herself. And there's something else: I'm in love with her niece. How do you think the family will feel about my part in all this?"

Webb was saved from answering by his bleeper. "May I use your phone? The station is trying to contact me."

In silence, Mark led him into the hall and indicated the instrument.

"Guv?" It was Jackson's voice, vibrating with excitement. "You're not going to believe this!"

"Try me," Webb invited grimly.

"Ted's been tailing this blue Renault. It was parked for over an hour outside a hairdresser's, so he was able to get a good look at it. And it's got scratches on it, in all the right places!"

"He hasn't lost it?" Webb asked sharply.

"No. The girl finally came out and drove it home. I'll give you three guesses where that is."

"Fauconberg House," said Webb flatly.

14

THEY HAD ARRIVED at Fauconberg House in convoy;
Webb and Jackson, Nina and Sally—it being sensible to have
woman officers on hand—and Mark Templeton, who'd insisted on accompanying them. They found the household in
the drawing-room with their pre-dinner drinks: Sir Julian and
Lady Harwood, their daughter, and Miss Matthews, whose
injured foot was supported with cushions.

Seeing Templeton with the police, Camilla paled and rose
to her feet. "Mark?" she faltered, and with set face he went
to her and took her hand.

Sir Julian said quietly, "Do you wish to see all of us, Chief
Inspector?"

"I'm afraid so, sir." Looking round the circle of anxious
faces, Webb was irresistibly reminded of the golden age de-
nouements of Agatha Christie, when the exuberant little Bel-
gian would gather the assembled suspects together in just
such a room. Life imitates art, he thought.

He cleared his throat. "Miss Harwood, you were observed
this afternoon driving a blue Renault 9. Can you confirm
this?"

Camilla, startled to find herself the centre of attention,
nodded. "Yes, that's right."

"Is it your car?"

"No," said Hattie Matthews in her deep voice, "it's
mine."

Webb let his breath out in a long sigh, studying the older

woman, whom he'd not met before. Large and ungainly, she seemed an odd companion for the pretty and petite Felicity. Her face, bare of make-up, was blotchily pale, the eyes puffy and red-rimmed, and her thin lank hair looked in need of washing.

He turned back to Camilla. "Have you borrowed it before?"

"A couple of times, yes; my own car's playing up a bit. I had Hattie's permission," she added, when Webb didn't immediately speak.

"Was Friday night one of those times?"

"Friday? I don't think so."

"It was the night before your aunt's last concert."

Camilla bit her lip. "I don't think so," she repeated.

He said to Hattie Matthews, "Then you drove it yourself that evening?"

She held his gaze. "No, I did not. I went to bed early, and so did Felicity; we made a point of doing, the night before a concert."

Webb turned to Lady Harwood. "Can you corroborate that, ma'am?"

"Yes; my sister-in-law went upstairs about nine, and Miss Matthews wasn't long after her."

Miss Matthews was watching him with a glint of triumph in her eyes. He said, "Had anyone else your permission to borrow the car?"

"No."

Sir Julian moved restlessly. "Chief Inspector, what's so important about the car?"

"It was outside Mr. Jessel's house about the time he was killed."

There was a deep, pulsating silence. The sudden tap on the door made them all jump.

"Come in," Lady Harwood called, her voice shaking. The maid put her head round the door, a frightened expression on her face.

"Excuse me, my lady, dinner's ready. Shall I hold it back a few minutes?"

"Yes please, Elsa."

The door closed. Hattie said stridently, "That's ridiculous. There must be some mistake."

"No mistake, Miss Matthews. It brushed against some thorns, leaving a trace of paint which I'm pretty sure will match the faint scratches along the side. An examination of the tyres should prove conclusive."

"Then some boys must have taken it joy-riding."

Webb raised an eyebrow. "And returned it afterwards? Where had you left it?"

"In the drive. There's no room in the garage."

He changed tack. "Miss Matthews, when did you first hear of the April Rainers?"

"When I saw the card from Felicity's bouquet."

"It meant nothing to you at the time?"

"On the contrary, it meant someone was threatening her."

"Did you show it to anyone?"

"No, I destroyed it at the first opportunity."

"Wasn't that rather foolish, when your friend's life might have been in danger?"

Hattie's eyes met his like small, muddy stones. "I didn't think that for a moment. There'd been letters before, and we always ignored them."

"So at the time you didn't take it seriously?"

"Of course not."

"But within a day or two—on Sunday, in fact—the newspapers were full of the April Rainers, and anyone who'd heard of them was asked to contact the police. Wouldn't that have been the natural thing to do?"

"All I saw of the Sunday papers were the review pages, and that afternoon I had my accident. What with having to go to the hospital, and my disappointment over the Scottish trip, I didn't give the card another thought."

"Perhaps because it had never existed?" Webb suggested, and felt everyone's surprise.

"I've no idea what you mean," Hattie said stolidly.

"Nor I," confessed Lady Harwood. "You owe us an explanation, Mr. Webb. Having told us Felicity received a note from these people, are you now saying she didn't?"

"I believe, Lady Harwood, that the card that so affected your sister-in-law was a perfectly harmless one, which wouldn't have had sinister implications to anyone else other than Miss Matthews."

Ignoring their exclamations and questions, Webb drew a piece of paper from his pocket. "Miss Matthews, I understand you arranged all Miss Harwood's concerts, saw to the bookings, and so on?"

"That's correct."

"Can you confirm, from memory, that she gave a performance in Chichester on the sixteenth of November last year?"

Hattie stared at him for a long moment. Then she said slowly, "Not from memory, no. It's possible."

"How about Cardiff, in June '85? Or Leeds, in March '83?"

"Where did you get those dates?" Mark interrupted. "Miss James—"

"That's right," Webb answered steadily. "I knew you'd been to all Miss Harwood's concerts, and I asked Miss James to check those particular dates with you."

"She didn't say it was for you!"

"You must blame me for that; I asked her not to."

Sir Julian said testily, "Chief Inspector, I haven't the faintest idea what's going on. What possible relevance have my sister's concert dates to the matter in hand?"

"A great deal, Sir Julian. They correspond very closely with murders committed by the April Rainers in those towns."

The three Harwoods were staring at him with complete

lack of comprehension, but Mark Templeton had gone white. He said, "Camilla, I swear—" and broke off.

Sir Julian shook his head helplessly. "You're going too fast. To go back to that note, you say it was quite innocuous after all?"

"Yes; I don't believe anyone tampered with the bouquets. The card which so upset your sister was, I suspect, simply a conventional one bearing good wishes and congratulations."

"Then why—?"

"It was signed by James Jessel." He looked across at Hattie. "Am I right?"

She did not reply, but Lady Harwood was frowning in bewilderment. "Whyever should that upset her? I know the poor man was to die soon afterwards, but Felicity couldn't have known that."

"But you see, Lady Harwood," Webb said softly, "I think she did."

Camilla said in a whisper, "Are you saying what I think you're saying?"

Out of the corner of his eye, Webb saw Mark Templeton's arm go round her. "Do any of you remember the title of the first piece of music she composed, when she was eight years old?" The Harwoods shook their heads. "Tell them, Miss Matthews."

Hattie Matthews held his gaze for two long minutes, during which no one moved. Was she ready to break yet, Webb wondered, or would he have to play cat-and-mouse a little longer? To his relief, he saw her take the decision, and some of the tension left her.

"Yes?" he prompted.

"It was called *April Rain*," she said.

Sir Julian was the first to find his voice. "But you're surely not insinuating that simply because—?"

"Not 'simply because,' Sir Julian. It's just one factor out of several that point in that direction."

Elizabeth Harwood said unbelievingly, "You're accusing *Felicity* of killing all those people?"

"Either her or Miss Matthews here. Or both of them."

Everyone turned to Hattie Matthews, who sat unmoving on the sofa, her flat face expressionless.

"And what are your other factors, Chief Inspector?" she challenged him.

"At first, we'd very little to go on. Two people were seen running out of Rankin Close after Baxter's death. They were thought to be men—one large and tall, one 'not more than a lad,' as the eye-witness put it. That was your first evening in Shillingham; perhaps you'd both retired early then, too.

"Our first real break was finding the paint fragments near Mr. Jessel's body. We established the make and year of the car they'd come from, and we knew that once we'd tracked it down we were likely to have the killer, because it was driven up onto the bank specifically to avoid Jessel's car and body.

"Later, when reports began to come in from other parts of the country, I remembered going to a concert in Chichester. And it suddenly struck me that all those towns had musical connections of some kind—festivals, or philharmonic orchestras, and so on. Which was why I asked for a list of Miss Harwood's engagements at the times of the murders. They coincided almost exactly.

"But it was the card you spoke of, Miss Matthews, that was your main mistake. It didn't ring true—it was too different from the established MO. But *something* had caused Miss Harwood to faint—we never bought the 'heat and excitement' theory. And looking through the list of those who'd sent flowers, I saw the name of James Jessel.

"Suppose he was the next intended victim, his death scheduled for only a couple of nights hence? The sudden shock of knowing he was there in the hall, that the flowers she held were from him, could have proved too much for her. She'd already have been in a highly charged emotional state after the concert, and that could have tipped her over the brink."

Webb looked round the circle of stunned faces, his eyes stopping at Hattie. "One thing I'd be interested to know, though, is the connection between all these deaths, and what possible motive you could have had."

There was another silence, and briefly he wondered if he'd been over-confident, if, after all, he wouldn't get a confession out of her. But then she began to speak.

"I remember, years ago, there was an item in the paper about someone who'd been fined for a parking offence. And Flick suddenly said, 'The whole system's crazy, Hattie. How can they punish people for parking and ignore the really terrible things—stunting someone's spiritual growth, crushing ambition, pinning down a lively spirit? Those are far more culpable, because they're crimes against the soul.' "

She shifted slightly, easing the pressure on her injured foot. "The family know how passionately she cared about fairness. She couldn't bear any kind of intimidation. That was how we met in the first place, when she rescued me from bullies on the playing field. We formed a secret society called 'The April Rainers,' with the object of sticking up for ourselves and anyone else who needed it. Flick said, 'There aren't eight of us, but I wrote *April Rain* when I was eight, so that'll have to do.'

"Years later, when the crusade really began, the number had a different significance. And again, it was Felicity's idea. We would rid the world of oppressive, cruel or sadistic people whom the law couldn't or wouldn't touch but who had made life hell for those around them. And to reinforce our name, we'd give them eight days' warning and limit our death-list to eight—for the April Rainers. The irony is that James Jessel *was* the eighth; there wouldn't have been any more."

"According to our calculations," Webb interrupted, "he was the seventh."

Hattie Matthews looked down at her folded hands. "The first," she said slowly, "was Felicity's father."

Sir Julian rose slowly to his feet, staring at her in horror. "What are you saying? Are you *mad?*"

Mark said into the silence, "I was told he died in a train crash."

Camilla moistened her lips. "Actually, I said 'rail accident.' He fell under a tube train at Oxford Circus during the rush hour."

With a sense of disbelief, Mark recalled the understated diary entry: "Spent the day with Hattie. When I got home, Mummy told me Daddy was dead."

Lady Harwood had also risen, and now moved to her husband's side, taking his hand. At that moment she seemed the stronger of the two. She addressed Hattie Matthews coldly. "Have you any proof at all of what you're saying?"

"Of course not. How could I have? But he'd refused, time and again, to allow Flick to study music, and kept insisting she should learn shorthand or 'something useful.' It was exactly the crushing of the spirit we'd vowed to fight against. Everything came to a head when she had the chance to spend the summer in Rome on a specialized course. She begged and pleaded to be allowed to go—it was during school holidays, after all—but her father refused to consider it. 'Over my dead body,' he said. And she realized that if she was to have any chance at all, that was how it had to be. Of course, we didn't send him a note, and obviously we didn't strangle him —the idea for all that came much later. But he was still our first—execution."

Webb broke the stunned silence. "How did you choose the rest of your victims?" he asked with genuine interest. "You can't have known them all personally."

"They weren't victims, Chief Inspector, they were perpetrators, people who had inflicted pain on others and for one reason or another got away with it. There was no shortage of candidates, I assure you. Think of all the sickening accounts you read. As to our method, we limited ourselves to areas where Flick was due to play and we'd a legitimate reason to be. I'd visit the location some weeks in advance, ostensibly to check bookings and hotels, meet managers and so on. It gave me the chance to study the target's movements and learn his or her routine, and since the executions were spread over several years, we never expected any connection to be made. Unfortunately, we didn't allow for either Mark Templeton's loyalty or the Chief Inspector's deductions."

She paused, but no one spoke. It occurred to Webb that, though she probably hadn't formulated the thought, she was pleading her own defence.

"Mental cruelty was our chief concern," she went on, "people whose hopes and dreams had been crushed—for example by shady businessmen like Thomas Raymond, who kept just inside the law. There was a link there, incidentally; our 'daily's' brother and his wife had been ruined by him."

"And James Jessel?" Webb prompted. "Why was he singled out?"

"Terence Denbigh, the journalist whose death he caused, was my uncle."

Something, Webb reflected bitterly, which had not come up during inquiries.

Hattie looked round the circle of closed faces. "As it happened, we were glad to have reached eight, because it was becoming an increasing strain. It had always been easier for Flick, who was psyched up for the concerts anyway. It carried her through, but I invariably went to pieces afterwards."

"You can't prove that Felicity was involved," Lady Harwood said again in her new, hard voice. "Quite apart from the ethics of it all, she simply wouldn't have the strength to—" She broke off, putting up a hand to shield her face.

"I did the actual killing, yes, but Flick acted as decoy. She pretended the car'd broken down, and got Jessel to peer into the bonnet. Then I came up behind him."

"And you're saying to commit both these murders you slipped out of the house without our knowing?" Sir Julian this time. He sounded dazed.

"Yes; I'd left the car outside instead of bringing it into the drive. We hoped no one would notice, but we'd an explanation ready if anyone had."

"Why alert your victims by sending notes?" Webb was still interested in the technicalities. "Didn't that add to the risk of discovery?"

"Since we weren't personally involved with them the risk was negligible, and we hoped they'd suffer some of the mental anguish they'd caused their victims. Oh, they might dismiss the note outwardly, but if they woke in the night, it wouldn't be a pleasant thing to brood on."

"You realize you're damning Felicity when she can't defend herself?" Lady Harwood again.

Hattie said impatiently, "What difference does it make? They can't hurt her now, and nothing matters to me any more. But if you still doubt me, there are signed confessions lodged with our solicitors. We wrote them some time ago, in case anyone else was ever charged."

Mark said in a low voice, "I wish I'd never met her. Most of all, I wish I'd never even considered the biography. Because of that, I've been used to point the finger at her, which is the last thing I'd have wanted."

"We know that," Camilla said softly.

Hattie gave a curious, choked laugh. "You all wondered why she'd turned down the professional biographers; well, now you know. We thought they'd be too thorough, go into everything too closely, and that could be dangerous. Templeton, on the other hand, was a competent reviewer, but also a devoted admirer. He seemed the ideal choice."

"And there I was, flattering myself." Mark's voice was bitter.

"I don't believe any of this!" Sir Julian announced jerkily. No one answered him, and Hattie Matthews merely shrugged her shoulders.

Webb stood up. "We took the precaution of bringing a wheelchair with us. If you'd bring it in, Miss Pierce?"

Sally left the room. Camilla turned in the circle of Mark's arm and began to cry softly. No one else moved until Sally returned, when she and Nina, assisted by Jackson, manoeuvred the heavy woman off the sofa and into the chair.

"You were very sure of yourself," she remarked, but put up no resistance. Webb's last impression, as he followed the police procession out of the room, was of Mark and the Harwoods staring after them.

The following evening, Hannah arrived at Webb's door with a basket of groceries.

"Thanks, love. This'll be the last time you'll have to shop for me."

"Till the next case!" she said. She went ahead of him into the kitchen, and emptied the goods out of her basket on to the table.

"It's time you had a clean newspaper in here," she commented, tipping the bag of carrots into the vegetable tray. Then her voice changed. "David, look at this."

He joined her, bending over to read the soiled paper which lined the basket.

MAN FOUND MURDERED IN RANKIN CLOSE, read one headline. And the other, alongside it: COMPOSER RETURNS TO SHILLINGHAM.

"Well, I'll be damned!" Webb said softly. "The answer was staring me in the face all the time!"

"I suppose the Abbey service will be cancelled?"

"It's highly likely. A shame, really, because whatever else she was, she was a superb musician."

"If she'd simply devoted herself to helping the oppressed, she'd have received nothing but praise. But she couldn't stop there, and the 'avenging angel' rôle was her downfall. It's odd, isn't it, how often genius is flawed, specially musical genius? Almost as though there's a price to pay for it."

Webb smiled and put an arm round her. "What are you on about now?"

"Well, for a start there was Beethoven, who began to go deaf at the age of twenty-seven. Can you imagine anything worse for a composer? Then Delius was blind and paralyzed for the last ten years of his life. Schumann went mad and died in an asylum after attempting suicide, and Mozart died at thirty-five and was buried in a pauper's grave. Even in this century, Lili Boulanger died of TB at the age of twenty-four. Does that convince you?"

"Painters haven't fared much better," Webb reminded her. "Aren't you glad I'm not a genius?"

"I'm serious."

"Oh, so am I. It's poor Sir Julian I'm most sorry for. His beloved sister's killed, and while he's still suffering from shock, he learns she was a murderess. What's more, she even murdered their father. I shouldn't be surprised if he chucks in his musical career after this."

"I should. To some extent, he was always in her shadow. When the grieving period's over, and the nine days' wonder, I think he'll emerge a greater conductor than ever."

"I hope you're right," Webb said, moving to the cabinet. "Now, I don't know about you, but I could use a drink."

"All right, I get the message. Case closed." She took the glass he handed her. "So what shall we drink to? Music? Genius? The Great Imponderables?"

"A few early nights!" said Webb with a grin.

ABOUT THE AUTHOR

Anthea Fraser was making up stories and poems before she could write. Her mother (who also wrote novels, four of which were published) took them down, illustrated them, and hung them round the nursery walls. Asked at the age of five what she wanted to be when she grew up, she answered without hesitation, "A mummy and an author." Her ambitions never changed, and she is thankful to have achieved them both.

All through her schooldays, first at prep school and then at Cheltenham Ladies' College, Anthea Fraser filled copious notebooks with poems and short stories, but she only began writing professionally when her younger daughter was fifteen months old. She then took a correspondence course with the London School of Journalism, during which she submitted one of her stories for a competition. It was a runner-up and through this she was contacted by Laurence Pollinger and had some dozen short stories published before trying her hand at a novel.

She wrote several romantic novels before submitting *Laura Possessed* for a competition for the best crime novel by a woman. It was on the short list until the last ten days of the competition, and afterwards proved very successful. (The definition of crime was wide-reaching and included the supernatural, which was the genre she chose and in which she continued for some years.)

She has now had twenty-three novels accepted, and her work has been translated into seven languages. *The April Rainers* is her sixth novel for the Crime Club.

She is Secretary of the Crime Writers' Association and a member of the Society of Women Writers and Journalists.